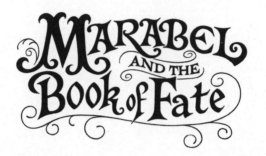

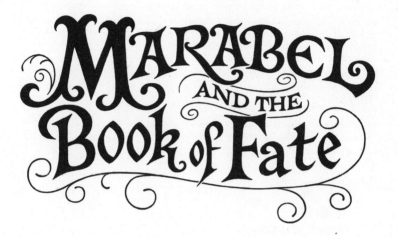

MARABEL AND THE Book of Fate

TRACY BARRETT

LITTLE, BROWN AND COMPANY

NEW YORK   BOSTON

Text copyright © 2018 by Alloy Entertainment, LLC
Interior Art copyright © 2018 by Sara Gianassi.

Cover design by Marcie Lawrence. Cover art copyright © 2018 by Sara Gianassi.
Cover copyright © 2018 by Hachette Book Group, Inc.

Little, Brown and Company
Hachette Book Group
1290 Avenue of the Americas, New York, NY 10104
Visit us at LBYR.com

Little, Brown and Company is a division of Hachette Book Group, Inc.
The Little, Brown name and logo are trademarks of Hachette Book Group, Inc.

The publisher is not responsible for websites (or their content) that are not owned by the publisher.

First Edition: February 2018

alloy**entertainment**

Produced by Alloy Entertainment
1325 Avenue of the Americas
New York, NY 10019
alloyentertainment.com

Book design by Mallory Griggs

Library of Congress Cataloging-in-Publication Data

Names: Barrett, Tracy, 1955- author.
Title: Marabel and the book of fate / by Tracy Barrett.
Description: First Edition. | New York; Boston: Little, Brown and Company, 2018. | Summary: When Princess Marabel's twin brother, Marco, is kidnapped on their thirteenth birthday, Princess Marabel must defy expectations and prophecies, leave the castle for the first time, and face great danger to rescue him.
Identifiers: LCCN 2017015323| ISBN 9780316433990 (hardback) | ISBN 9780316433983 (ebook) | ISBN 9780316554961 (library edition ebook)
Subjects: | CYAC: Adventure and adventurers—Fiction. | Princesses—Fiction. | Brothers and sisters—Fiction. | Twins—Fiction. | Kidnapping—Fiction. | Prophecies—Fiction. | Fantasy. | BISAC: JUVENILE FICTION / Fantasy & Magic. | JUVENILE FICTION / Action & Adventure / General. | JUVENILE FICTION / Girls & Women. | JUVENILE FICTION / Fairy Tales & Folklore / General. | JUVENILE FICTION / Social Issues / Self-Esteem & Self-Reliance.
Classification: LCC PZ7.B275355 Mar 2018 | DDC [Fic]—dc23
LC record available at https://lccn.loc.gov/2017015323

ISBN: 978-0-316-43399-0 (hardcover), 978-0-316-43398-3 (ebook)
Printed in the United States of America

LSC-C
10 9 8 7 6 5 4 3 2 1

To all those who have the courage
to create their own destiny

1

arabel of Magikos wasn't the kind of princess who normally went on adventures. For one thing, she didn't have a wicked stepmother who made her work all the time or plotted to kill her out of envy of her beauty. Her stepmother, who was actually very nice, treated Princess Marabel exactly the same way she treated her own royal children.

Also, Marabel wasn't the youngest and most beautiful of three sisters. She was the oldest girl in her family (her twin brother, Marco, was only one minute older), and while she was pretty enough, she had ordinary brown hair and freckles, not the golden curls or raven tresses that the more adventure-prone princesses always seemed to have.

Marabel's parents knew only one fairy socially, and she was not the type to put a curse on a baby to prick her finger on a spinning wheel or to drop toads from her mouth when she spoke. In any case, this fairy had been properly invited to the twins' christening and had given each baby a lumpy wool blanket she had crocheted herself.

It was highly unlikely that Marabel would be captured by a dragon and rescued by a prince—or that her hand would be given in marriage as a reward. Her father, King Matthew, would probably grant her hand to the first prince who asked for it as long as he seemed nice, instead of demanding that his new son-in-law be a dragon slayer. The few dragons left in Magikos lived in a wildlife preserve. Visitors sometimes toasted marshmallows in their fiery breath, even though signs sternly cautioned people: STAY IN CARRIAGES. NOT RESPONSIBLE FOR INJURY CAUSED BY MAGICAL BEASTS. The survivors would bring home toy dragons wearing little shirts that said things like "My parents went to the Magikos Wildlife Park and all they got me was this dragon."

Moreover, the Book of Fate, which told important Magikians what their futures held, didn't say a word about

Princess Marabel. Her family's pages mostly talked about the Chosen One—her twin brother, Prince Marco—the One all Magikians had been waiting and hoping for, for a thousand years.

The Book didn't mention the Chosen One having a twin sister. Everyone assumed that Marabel was merely an afterthought, an unimportant footnote.

So when adventure came to Princess Marabel, at first she didn't recognize it.

On the afternoon of the day adventure found her, Marabel was practicing her sword fighting. Marco's fencing lessons with old Lucius took place out in the stable yard, but Marabel's lessons were held in a seldom-visited tower. That way, she wouldn't risk being caught by her parents, who insisted that for Marabel, sword fighting was improper and a waste of time. After all, they reminded her, she would never need to know how to use a weapon.

But Marabel loved fencing, and Lucius seemed happy to teach her. Right now, he faced her in a fighter's stance—knees bent in a crouch, weight on his toes. Marabel danced lightly back and forth, her wooden practice sword raised as she looked for an opening.

Aha! She leaped forward and thrust her sword through a gap in Lucius's leather armor.

Clunk! The old knight's sword bonked her head with a jolt that made her teeth clash together. Marabel thought she would faint. She swayed, the sword dangling from her hand, lights dancing in front of her eyes. Luckily, Lucius's sword was made of wood, too.

"Ha!" Lucius's cracked voice was triumphant. "Your brother would never have fallen for that!"

The taunt energized Marabel. Instantly, her vision cleared and her grip tightened, and she lunged again at Lucius. He swiveled to put his shield between them, but at the last instant she dodged behind him and whacked the backs of his knees with her sword.

The knight's feet flew out from under him and he crashed to the straw-covered floor. He lay motionless on his back, his short gray beard pointing at the ceiling.

Marabel lowered her sword and waited for him to get up.

He didn't move, not even a little. His eyes remained shut.

"Lucius?"

No answer.

Warily, expecting his hand to shoot out and grab her

ankle, Marabel circled his motionless body. She prodded him with the tip of her sword. "Lucius?"

Still nothing.

"What's the matter? Old marsh frog needs a little nap?"

The corner of his mouth twitched.

Relief flooded Marabel. If she'd hurt Lucius—her only true friend besides Ellie—she'd never forgive herself.

Marabel was suddenly aware of her aches and pains. Her head was sore where Lucius had thwacked her, and her wrist was already showing a bruise from an earlier blow.

"You know," she said, pulling off her helmet and shaking free her hair, damp with sweat, "I'm almost as good as Marco now. I'd be *better* than Marco if I could practice out in the open like he does."

Lucius sat up and grunted, rubbing his back with one hand.

"And especially if I had a *real* fencing master."

He chuckled, as she knew he would.

Marabel uncorked the flask of bluefruit juice that she had brought as a treat for Lucius, knowing it was his favorite. When the sweet aroma drifted out, the old man grinned.

"Help me up, Princess." Lucius had lived in the palace since before Marabel was born, but he still spoke with the soft accent of the marshland where he'd grown up, making his last word sound like "brinzezz."

She waved the bottle at him, trying to look stern. "Do you promise it's not a trick to pull me down?"

"I swear on the Book."

Marabel set the flask on the bench and hoisted the old man to his feet. Nobody, not even Lucius, would break an oath made on the Book of Fate.

"Where did you learn that move?" He settled next to her on the bench with a tired groan.

She shrugged. "Just came to me." She laid the sword crosswise on her lap. She couldn't help feeling smug about tricking him.

"I didn't injure you, did I?" Lucius asked. "Let me see."

Marabel bent her head and pointed at the sore spot. She winced in anticipation as his long fingers parted her hair, but he touched her so lightly that it didn't hurt. Ellie always said that Lucius's touch was soothing. She was right.

"There's nothing there, Princess," Lucius said with a smile and a pat on the shoulder.

Marabel straightened and felt for herself. Sure enough, no lump. Huh. He must not have hit her as hard as she'd thought.

She wiped the sweat off her forehead and picked up the flask of juice again. But Lucius put out a restraining hand as she raised it to her lips. "Best not."

She lowered it. "But why?"

"Don't want to turn your teeth blue, do you? The queen wouldn't like that, not right before the banquet."

The banquet! Marabel thrust the flask into the old knight's hands and shot to her feet. With a wail of dismay, she tore out the door and sped down the spiral staircase. Plague, plague, *plague* it! How could she have let the time get away from her like that? The banquet was all her parents had been talking about for months. All anyone in the kingdom had been talking about for *years*, it seemed.

Marabel and Marco were turning thirteen at precisely thirteen minutes past thirteen o'clock on this, the thirteenth day of the thirteenth month. Or rather, Marco was turning thirteen at thirteen minutes past thirteen; Marabel would have to wait another minute for her own birthday.

Not that anyone would notice when Marabel came of age at 13:14. Everyone in the entire kingdom, from the Purple Ocean all the way to the Impassable Forest, would be shouting and beating on drums and setting off fireworks, celebrating the Chosen One. Meanwhile, Princess Marabel would sit forgotten at the banquet table.

And even worse, now she was going to be late. She knew what the courtiers would say—that she was irresponsible. Impulsive. Easily distracted from her royal duties. Oh, plague it!

Marabel was paying so little attention to where she was going that when she rounded a corner at top speed, she ran right into something that let out a startled "Oof!"

It was her father, followed by her stepmother. They were already dressed for the banquet. The surprise on King Matthew's face was instantly replaced by his usual look of disappointment. Marabel tried not to let his expression hurt her feelings, but her father's annoyance still stung.

Her father asked, "What are you doing with that—that *weapon*?"

Marabel was baffled for a moment, but then realized she was still clutching the battered old practice sword.

"And you're wearing a red garb?" the queen added. "Have you been fencing again?"

Knights, even student knights, always wore red. It was supposed to keep them from seeing their own blood if they were wounded.

The queen shook her head at her stepdaughter's most recent lapse in propriety. "Fencing isn't ladylike, dear." Marabel had to use all her strength not to roll her eyes.

Her father stretched out his hand. "Give me the weapon."

Marabel took a step back. What could she do? She couldn't say it belonged to Lucius—her father would instantly dismiss the old man for teaching her sword fighting. Lucius would have to go back to the marsh, where the damp would make his rheumatism so bad that he wouldn't even be able to walk. But neither could she let the king take away the practice sword. He would be sure to toss it in the fire.

"Well?" he demanded.

Marabel opened her mouth, without knowing what she was going to say, but then a merry voice exclaimed, "My sword!" Marabel spun around. There, dressed in his banquet finery and wearing his best crown, stood Marco.

"*Your* sword?" the queen asked.

Marco took the sword from Marabel and made a few passes in the air. With a private grin at her, he said, "Thanks for fetching it for me, Mara."

Marabel smiled back at her brother, even as she tried to ignore a small twinge. Once again, the Chosen One had saved the day.

Being with Marco always made Marabel think of her black-and-white pony after she'd been basking in the sun. The pony's black hair soaked up all the heat, leaving her white spots cool. In the same way, Marco soaked up everyone's attention, leaving Marabel out in the cold. He didn't *try* to be the center of attention; it happened just because he was Marco, always sweet, always kind, always fun to be with, and so handsome, with his big brown eyes and his glossy golden hair, like their father. He already looked the part of a future king.

But for once, Marabel was glad all the attention was on her brother. The king straightened Marco's crown while the queen tucked a strand of his shining hair behind one ear. They'd completely forgotten about Marabel, so she slipped behind the king, crossing her eyes and sticking out her tongue at Marco to make him laugh. He let out a snort, which he quickly disguised as a cough.

"You're not coming down with a cold, darling, are you?" the queen asked him anxiously.

Marabel didn't wait to hear his answer, but sped away down the corridor. She let herself into her bedchamber. The door had been left ajar, which meant that Ellie was already there. She was uncomfortable in small spaces and was always uneasy in a room that had its door closed.

"Oh, Marabel! You're late." Marabel could sense Ellie's nervousness. "I've filled your bath. Hop in."

Even though Ellie was Marabel's best friend, she had been bossing Marabel around ever since they were seven, when she had become Marabel's personal maid. Marabel usually resisted Ellie's orders, but now she meekly stripped off her filthy garb and eased herself into the steaming tub.

She gritted her teeth as she lowered her sore wrist into the water.

While Marabel scrubbed herself, Ellie worked a handful of soapweed into her hair, clucking as bits of straw and dirt floated out. Marabel rinsed off and stepped out of the tub, dripping, and Ellie wrapped her in a manticore skin. It was luxuriously soft—a new one, Marabel noticed. This was an indulgence even for the royal family, since manticores shed their skin only once every three years.

"Where did you get this new skin from?" she asked as Ellie helped her dry her hair. "It's so soft!"

"I have my ways," Ellie said with a grin. "It's possible that it was intended for someone else, and it, um, found its way into your chamber instead."

Marabel suspected that the manticore skin was supposed to go to Marco, but she was soothed, just a little, by Ellie's thoughtfulness.

"Time for your new garb," Ellie said when Marabel was dry. She held up the garment. It was made of shimmering fabric that changed from blue to white, then to yellow and then to green, and back to white again in the wavering torchlight. Like all garbs, it consisted of trousers worn with a hooded tunic that flowed past the wearer's waist. It had pockets, folds, and tucks that must have had a purpose once, but that was now long forgotten.

The hood on this particular garb wasn't for use—no one would expose such an expensive fabric to rough weather. But every Magikian garb was worn with a hooded tunic, because that had been the style at the time of King Manfred, Marabel's many-times great-grandfather, and it had never changed. It never occurred to anyone to question the custom, just as they never questioned that the name of every member of the royal family must start with "Ma"—the queen's name had been changed from Alexandra to Maggie when she married King Matthew—or any of the other rules from the Book of Fate that governed their lives.

Ellie helped Marabel step into the garb. It fit perfectly.

"Let me see your wrist," Ellie said.

Marabel held out her right arm.

"No, the other one." The one with the bruise from Lucius's sword.

Ellie frowned, and then fastened a broad bracelet made of stones from the bottom of the Purple Ocean on Marabel's wrist. Now no one at the banquet would ask Marabel how she'd gotten hurt, which would have led to trouble. It was the perfect solution, one that only Ellie would think of.

Marabel flung her arms around Ellie's waist and hugged

her so tightly that the other girl squeaked. "Thank you," Marabel whispered. Ellie returned the hug before gently freeing herself from the princess's embrace.

"Now, we have just enough time to do your hair," Ellie said. Marabel sat down at her dressing table and watched in the mirror as Ellie's swift fingers moved in and out of her damp tresses. It took longer than usual, since Marabel had only a regular mirror these days. The magical talking mirror that gave grooming and dress suggestions had become so annoying that Ellie had gotten rid of it.

Marabel looked down at her lap. She didn't want to see her nervousness reflected, even in this ordinary mirror.

Ellie gave Marabel a comforting smile as she patted a stray lock into one of Marabel's braids. "What do you think?" she asked.

Marabel thought she looked better than usual in her new clothes and with her hair pinned up out of her face. But then she thought of the other princesses who'd been invited to the party. They would certainly be wearing something much fancier than a Magikian garb, and their hair would be adorned with diamonds and emeralds instead of the flowers Ellie had woven into hers. Marabel was usually asked to other princesses' birthday parties, but she had the feeling that their parents included her merely to be polite.

The other girls mostly ignored Marabel while they chatted among themselves, only occasionally seeming to remember she was there. Marabel dreaded having to talk with them even more than she dreaded being ignored.

She shrugged. "It's all right, I guess. It's not like anybody will be looking at me."

Ellie's face fell.

"Oh, I didn't mean that you didn't do a good job," Marabel said hurriedly. It was bad enough being a second-rate princess—what must it be like to be the *maid* of a second-rate princess? "You did. You always do. And I know you know how it feels to be ignored."

Ellie looked a little less hurt.

Encouraged, Marabel went on, "If only you could come to the party! It would be so much fun if you were there, too. Remember that state banquet when we were five? You got me into trouble by making faces at me every time that silly princess from Norumbega said something mean—"

"And you laughed each time, and everyone thought you were laughing at *her*!" Ellie said, smiling at the memory.

"That princess got so *mad*! And remember—"

The tinny blast of a trumpet from the banquet hall interrupted her. Ellie gently pushed Marabel to the door.

"It's all right. I'll come to the hall to help my mother with the little ones after your father gives his speech. I don't want to have to sit through *that*!"

"I'll take notes on the speech and recite it to you before bed tonight," Marabel said. "That will be sure to put us both to sleep!" And she hurried down the corridor, feeling cheered by the sound of Ellie's warm laughter echoing off the cold stone walls.

2

arabel looked down the lofty stairway into the banquet hall. The spacious room was filled with highly polished long tables, hundreds of glowing candles, and towering flower arrangements that scented the air with heavy perfume. Groups of people dotted the floor, talking and laughing.

Marabel overheard snatches of instructions as guests waited to make their way through the magic detector at the door: "Use up any magic you brought with you before you get to the front of the line.... Shoes off, please, madam.... Please deposit that charm in the tray and come through again. . . ." The detector was intended to keep out magical beings, and from what the guards were saying, it also kept out anything magical that a non-magic person might be carrying, such as a potion or a wish.

A confused-looking old man—tall and very thin, with white, wispy hair, his long black shoes clutched in one hand—triggered the detector. Lights flashed and a horn sounded. A guard lifted his voice over the alarm. "Sorry, sir, no magic allowed in the palace except charms and spells weighing less than three ounces."

Suddenly, Marabel noticed a woman in a green garb. The woman snuck around the crowd and slipped into the hall, bypassing the magic detector. Nobody else seemed to notice her. It was probably nothing—the woman was probably just impatient and wanted to get to the party. But just in case something wrong was going on, Marabel hurried down the staircase to warn the chief guard.

His expression showed a hint of impatience as Marabel lamely finished her account with, "I thought maybe someone should know. . . ."

"Thank you, Your Highness." The guard bowed. "We'll be sure to look into it."

Marabel could tell he hadn't taken her seriously, and

for a moment thought of reporting it to Lucius. But he was busy, and the guard knew what he was doing—didn't he?

She glanced around the room and spotted the Princess Table, draped in royal blue and gold, a crown of lilies in the center. Four princesses were seated near Marabel's throne at the head of the table. They leaned close together, whispering about something that made their eyes shine with glee. Marabel tried to relax as she headed in their direction. She felt a pang of envy as she passed her little half brother and half sisters giggling with their nanny, Ellie's mother, Poppy. The children were thrilled to be up past their bedtime.

As she reached her throne, Marabel smiled nervously and said, "Welcome!" The conversation stopped abruptly and all four princesses jumped up and dropped into deep curtseys. Marabel did the same gracefully, silently thanking Poppy for the endless drills in curtseying and dancing that had started when she and Ellie were so young they had barely been able to walk.

Marabel inquired politely after her guests' journeys. Magikos was on a peninsula jutting out westward into the Purple Ocean. The Impassable Forest cut it off from the Barrens and the rest of the mainland to the east. The princesses had all come by sea, except Princess Ginevra of Norumbega, who'd flown in on an enchanted swan.

Once pleasantries were finished, Ginevra continued the story that Marabel had interrupted. "And so when the prince arrived, she took one look at him and said, 'It's true he looks like a frog, but I'm certainly not going to kiss him to find out what happens!'" The three other princesses burst out laughing.

"Didn't that hurt the prince's feelings?" Marabel said.

An uncomfortable silence fell, until Ginevra said stiffly, "If he couldn't take a joke, he should have stayed home."

It didn't sound like a joke to Marabel. *I wish . . .* she started to think, but hastily changed her thought to: *If only I could leave.*

Everyone in Magikos knew better than to say, or even think, "I wish." Instead, children learned to say "If only." But people sometimes forgot. Once, Marabel was invited to Norumbega for Princess Ginevra's birthday. She gave Ginevra a present that, it turned out, Ginevra didn't want. Ginevra lost her temper and said, "I wish I just had people I liked at my party!" Instantly, Marabel found herself back home, a bite of cake still on her fork, a party hat still balanced crookedly on top of her crown. Her only comfort was that someone must have purchased that wish at great expense, and Ginevra had wasted it on sending Marabel back to Magikos, which was where she wanted to be anyway.

One of the girls asked Princess Felicia, "What ever happened with that curse on your little cousin?"

"Your cousin was cursed?" Marabel asked Felicia.

"Why, yes, at his baby shower. Don't you—oh, that's right. You weren't there." Marabel tried not to feel hurt by this reminder of how she'd been left out. It wasn't like this was the first time, after all.

"You see," Felicia said, "my aunt and uncle have only twelve golden goblets, and they had invited thirteen fairies. They never thought all thirteen would accept, but they did." She put on a look of false modesty, but it really *was* impressive that thirteen fairies would attend a baby shower.

"Oh! It was *so* scary when the thirteenth one appeared!" one of the princesses added.

"Anyway," Felicia went on, "at first she didn't seem upset about having to drink from a silver goblet instead of a gold one, but once the rest of the fairies had given their presents, she said, 'Here's my gift to the child, and one that will surely gladden his parents' hearts. The baby will never cry.'"

"That doesn't sound like a curse to me," Marabel said.

"Oh, but it is." Felicia looked dubiously at the food in front of her. "My aunt and uncle never know if he's hungry or tired or wet, or if he's woken up in the night, because he never makes a sound. So they have four nursemaids who take turns with him around the clock, and they're always trying to feed him or change him or put him to bed in case he's unhappy and they don't know it. They can't *wait* until he learns to talk."

Servants crossed the stone floor with the birthday cakes, each adorned with thirteen long, flaming candles, and deposited them on the tables. The huge one set in front of Marco was covered in white icing.

A maid placed a second cake, also frosted in white, on the Princess Table.

The king's chancellor read a proclamation from a long scroll. He declared to great cheers that, henceforth, the thirteenth day of the thirteenth month would be a national holiday. A group of blue-garbed priests recited the portion of the Book of Fate that prophesied the coming of the Chosen One. The words were so familiar that all the Magikians followed along, even though it was written in an ancient language that hardly anyone understood anymore:

For, lo! When the Chosen One is recognized, what was broken shall be repaired and harmony shall rule o'er the land. The Chosen One's valor will turn a great threat away from the kingdom and all shall rejoice.

Familiar though the text was, the words had a special

meaning on this fateful day. Marabel glanced at Marco. He listened, his eyes shining.

The passage from the Book went on and on that way, talking vaguely about peace and unity. Nobody was sure exactly what it meant, although everyone agreed that the "all shall rejoice" part sounded pretty good.

Prince Malcolm, Marabel's little half brother, whined to Poppy, who tried unsuccessfully to keep him quiet. Poppy had her hands full with Maisie and Maria, the younger princesses, so Marabel motioned for the boy to join her.

Malcom trotted over, his hard little boots *rat-tatting* on the stone floor, and Marabel lifted him onto her lap. She bounced the squirming boy on her knee, whispering in his ear that he was a brave knight galloping through the forest.

Malcolm usually loved when Marabel played with him, but this time he wriggled out of her hold and nearly fell. He sent up a piercing wail that made the priests fall silent, her stepmother half rise from her throne, and every eye in the room turn in their direction.

Or almost every eye. Even in her embarrassment, even as a wailing Malcolm went running to Marco, who pulled the little boy on his lap and kissed the top of his head, Marabel noticed something odd at a table in the farthest corner. The bumbling old man and the woman in the green garb were engaged in a private conversation. Their concentration was so intense that Marabel could swear the air around them crackled and sparked.

She glanced at the huge countdown clock that had been set up to mark the exact moment Marco turned thirteen, just as King Matthew stood up to make the final speech. Only thirteen minutes left.

"As you all know," the king began, "no one expected Marco to be born on this day, thirteen years ago. There was still more than a month left before our first child was supposed to arrive, so Queen Marianna was alone in her chamber with the royal nanny." Poppy stood and curtsied, and then took her seat again. When Marabel's mother had died a few weeks after their birth, Poppy had practically raised the twins herself.

"As soon as the royal doctor realized what was happening, we hastened to the chamber, and at exactly thirteen minutes past thirteen, Prince Marco appeared. So there can be no doubt"—the king looked around sternly, as though daring someone to contradict him—"that Marco is the Chosen One foretold by the great Magikian Book of Fate. His dear mother..." He choked a little, and Queen Maggie laid a gentle hand on his. Marabel blinked back a tear. After a moment, the king continued, "His dear mother would be so happy to know that he has grown to be all that a parent could wish." He raised his head and his voice strengthened. "And tonight, at thirteen minutes past the thirteenth hour, we will celebrate my son's thirteenth birthday and his destiny as the next leader of our great kingdom."

Everyone cheered and leaped to their feet, Marabel shouting the loudest of all. Marco would be a wonderful king. He was kind and gentle and honest. He would rule justly and everyone would love him, just as Marabel did, and she would do her best to be his most loyal subject.

Marco looked up at their father and said something quietly. The king leaned over. "What? Oh yes, of course. I was just about to say that." He straightened and faced the crowd again. "Today we *also* celebrate the coming of age of my oldest daughter, Princess Marabel." Marabel stood and curtsied, waving to the guests as they clapped politely. Her father smiled vaguely in her direction, and she sat down again.

"And so," King Matthew said, raising his glass of bluefruit wine, "please join me in congratulating Marco, my dear son and your future king, on his coming of age and the expectation of fulfilling the great prophecy." He raised his glass, and so did everyone else.

Marabel glanced up at the high dais where her brother sat between the king and queen, with Malcolm on his lap.

The little boy was sucking his finger and leaning against Marco contentedly, his eyelids drooping in sleep. Marabel couldn't bear the look of pride in her father's eyes, a look that she never saw when he was talking about her. She abruptly stood, and the other princesses looked at her in bewilderment. "'Scuse me," Marabel mumbled. "I've just got to—"

She bolted for the grand staircase. She didn't know where she was going; she only knew she had to get out of that hot room, heavy with the smell of spice cake, the room where she was reminded that she was nobody.

She had almost reached the top of the stairs when a scream rang out from the banquet hall and a green light exploded behind her.

Marabel whipped around in shock.

A sickly color bathed every inch of the hall. Everyone and everything had stopped moving. The candle flames were frozen on their wicks, and a stream of water, half-poured from a silver pitcher, remained suspended over a goblet. It looked like a greenish crystal waterfall. People were trapped in whatever position they had been in when that light flashed. Marco sat with his head bent over Malcolm's. A little dog balanced on its hind legs, its mouth open and ready to snap at a bone that hung in midair.

The countdown clock had stopped just short of the thirteenth minute of the thirteenth hour.

What could have happened to make even time *stand still?*

Were people even breathing? Marabel couldn't tell from this distance. She put her hand over her mouth to hold back an anguished cry.

Then two figures rose from the table in the far corner: the woman in the green garb and the old man, his bewildered expression replaced by a look of lively intelligence. Marabel cowered at the top of the stairs and prayed they wouldn't notice her.

The woman dropped an exaggerated curtsey to the royal table. "It appears that my invitation to your son's birthday party got lost in transit," she said to King Matthew, whose eyes flashed in unmistakable rage, even while he remained frozen in place. "I took the liberty of coming anyway, and I've had *such* a lovely time." She strode up to the dais and threw back her hood. "Excuse me if I gloat, but you'll have to admit that I've won this time, Brother."

Brother? Marabel clapped her hand over her mouth to keep in a yelp. It dawned on her who the woman must be: her aunt Mab, her father's older sister, who had been banished from Magikos when Marabel and Marco were babies—for what crime, Marabel had never been told.

Now Mab ruled the Desolate Barrens. The Barrens had been created thousands of years earlier by the great wizard Callum. He built a magical wall to separate the Barrens from the western part of the country, where the royal family lived. He exiled the Evils—witches, magicians, ogres, and the like—to the other side of the Wall. Though most people still considered the Barrens a part of Magikos, no member of the royal family had ever showed much interest in that side of the kingdom—until Mab took over and proclaimed herself their queen.

"Mab," the old man said urgently. "Save your triumph for another time and grab the boy. The spell will only last another few minutes, and I won't be able to recharge for at least an hour."

The woman ignored him and kept her focus on King Matthew.

"You know what I want," she said to the king. "You have a thrennight to give me rule over all of Magikos. I will consider your refusal to do so an open declaration of war—and, Brother, you don't want to go to war with me. You'll never win and you'll never see your son again—at least not in any form that you'd recognize."

Marabel felt her blood run cold.

Her aunt went on, "My friend Veneficus here is quite

adept at turning boys into frogs and toads, and he's been looking forward to a chance to branch out into something else. How do you think your firstborn would look as a snake?"

What? Turn her brother into a snake? Declare war on Magikos? It was too horrible even to imagine.

Marabel thought fast. Her father was frozen, and so were all the soldiers. It was up to her to find some way to stop Mab from taking her brother and starting a war.

With her heart thumping so loud she was sure the people below could hear it, Marabel crawled out of hiding. She kept low to the ground to stay out of sight.

The king's hand twitched—slowly, with obvious effort. The strange green light was starting to thin, like a morning mist burned off by the sun.

As Marabel crept down the stairs, Mab jumped lightly onto the dais. She pried Marco's arms open and removed little Malcolm from his hold. Veneficus climbed up next to her, and together they picked up Marco. His head tilted forward as though he were still whispering to Malcolm, and his knees were bent at right angles. Despite her threats, Mab handled the prince gently. The two intruders carried Marco down the steps. The magic that had made everyone freeze in place must have been starting to fade, because one of his arms flopped down and swung back and forth. As Mab and Veneficus turned to get through the door, Marabel caught a glimpse of his face. His eyes held confusion, which was swiftly replaced with anger and determination.

Marabel leaped up and howled, "Noooooo!"

Veneficus looked startled, but Mab's eyes narrowed in anger. She nearly dropped Marco as she freed one hand and grabbed something from the bag slung over her shoulder. Marabel barely managed to dodge the bright emerald-colored blast that flew from her aunt's hand. She scrambled to her feet, but before she could take even one more step, Veneficus and Mab had hurried out of the palace and disappeared into the darkness. The door slammed shut behind them.

"Marco!" Marabel flew down the rest of the stairs. She dodged around people who were starting to move again, barely noticing that the candle flames were shimmering once more. She flung open the outer door, only to leap backward with a gasp.

A huge, scaly face, mottled brown and gray, blocked her path and glared at her with red eyes, smoke curling lazily from its nostrils. The hideous creature grinned, showing ridiculously long teeth, and then opened its mouth wide. It was a dragon—an obviously *wild* dragon, not one of the tame ones from the preserve—stretched out on the draw-bridge, preventing anyone from giving chase.

Marabel slammed the door and leaned against it, breathing hard. A distant cry came from outside, and she recognized her twin's voice.

"Marco!" she screamed again, and pounded her fists on the door in frustration. "Marco!"

But there was no answer.

3

A sudden clanging made everyone jump, but it was only the countdown clock, which had stirred to life and reached 13:13. Confetti popped out of holders in the walls and multicolored balloons dropped from the ceiling.

Marabel took off running, dodging guests and servants who blinked as though waking from a long sleep. She knocked a pile of plates off a table and hardly noticed the crash when they hit the stone floor. All she could think of was getting to Marco.

She tore up the staircase and flew down the corridor.

It seemed agonizingly long until she reached a door that led outside. She yanked it open.

This time, it was not a dragon, but a giant, that faced her. Its knees were at her eye level, but she didn't look up to see the rest of it. She stumbled back inside and frantically pushed the door shut. She ran toward another door, her breath coming in gasps.

Just before she reached it, a guard stepped in front of her. "Stop!" he commanded, hastily adding, "Your Highness."

"Let me pass!" Marabel cried.

"It's no use, miss," he said. "There's an ogre out there. There's an Evil at every exit from the palace. I can't let you through."

"But you *have* to!" she cried, and tried to push past him. He held her firmly at arm's length.

"Marabel!" It was Ellie. Marabel turned her head, and the guard released her. Ellie ran up and grabbed her in a tight hug. After a moment, Ellie whispered, "Be brave, Princess. Let's go back to the banquet hall and see what we can do to help."

Marabel perched on the edge of her chair and tried to appear calm, but she burned with worry and impatience.

Why wasn't anybody *doing* anything? They only had a thrennight—thirteen short days—to get her brother back. Surely her father would announce that his soldiers would fight off the Evils blocking the doors, and depart on a rescue quest.

The room buzzed with confusion as everyone tried to understand what had happened. King Matthew called out, "Please stay calm! The palace guards have the situation under control!" Marabel doubted this, but it seemed to reassure the guests, who settled back into their chairs. The king stood at his throne on the high dais. The queen was still seated. The throne in the middle, where Marco had sat, was empty and forlorn. Marabel couldn't bear to look at it.

"Honored guests—my apologies for this disgraceful intrusion," the king continued, his voice a tad unsteady. "Tradition dictates that we use a Ritual of Consultation to find a solution to our problem. The Book of Fate will surely tell us what must happen in this time of trouble. Magikos will not rest until we know the fate of the Chosen One." The king clapped his hands twice and sat down on his throne.

Marabel tried to console herself with the thought that, of course, the Book would tell them what was fated to happen. It listed all important events, and what could be more important than the disappearance of the Chosen One just as he was about to come of age? Surely the priests and priestesses would find out what they were supposed to do. From the dais, her stepmother gave her a reassuring smile. Marabel returned it as well as she could, but inside, she ached to leap on a horse and take off into the night.

The thirteen priests and priestesses of Magikos, led by High Priestess Symposia, marched down the staircase. Everyone fell silent and waited.

The priests and priestesses chanted. Marabel tried not to scream with impatience. She had heard of the Ritual of Consultation, but she'd never seen one performed before. There hadn't been a problem big enough for a Ritual since before she was born. The Book had told about other important things that happened—it had said that a great calamity would befall the royal family, for example, and Marabel and Marco's mother had died. But since no one knew what the calamity was going to be, they hadn't known how to try to prevent it.

Whenever calamities were prevented, the Book didn't mention them. When Marabel was little, there had been a drought that caused the farmers' crops to fail. Before anyone could panic, King Matthew had thrown open the doors to the royal granary and allowed everyone to take what they needed. Afterward, Marabel had overheard her father asking why the Book hadn't mentioned the drought. High Priestess Symposia had said that His Majesty, in his wisdom, had solved the problem before it had reached the necessary severity for inclusion in the Book (she always talked like that).

Another time, a troupe of half-human, half-horse creatures who called themselves "centaurs" had gone rampaging through the countryside. The guards caught their leader and told him that he and his friends didn't belong in Magikos. The centaurs were very apologetic, and the royal navy sailed them to their home, a distant and beautiful land called Mythikos. After their return, the sailors said they had seen more centaurs there, and some creatures that were even stranger, like mischievous half-goat people. Once the centaurs were gone, things in Magikos went back to normal. Still, Marabel and Marco often wished that the exciting strangers would return.

At the time, there had been some discontented murmurs asking why the priests hadn't warned them about the centaurs. Symposia reminded the people that the Book couldn't account for every thunderstorm or flood! It would be volumes and volumes long if it did. The drought was just another weather occurrence, and the centaur "invasion" was no real invasion, just a case of some travelers getting lost. The king had solved both problems before disaster struck.

Finally, a bell rang solemnly to indicate that the Ritual was beginning. At last, they would get started.

One of the priests burned a dried plant, and soon, thick, stinking smoke filled the banquet hall. The rest of the priests chanted in the Book's ancient language. Marabel had studied Old Magikian, but she understood only some simple words, like "help" and "please."

One priest covered Symposia's eyes with a blindfold while another flipped the Book's pages back and forth. The paper made a dry rustling sound, and Marabel caught the sweet vanilla scent of old books. One of the priestesses sneezed at the cloud of dust that flew out of the faded paper. The people in the banquet hall murmured and shifted their weight in anticipation. Maria, the youngest Magikian princess, whimpered sleepily as Poppy carried her out. Ellie led a drowsy Malcolm and Maisie up the stairs. As Ellie went by, she cast an encouraging smile at Marabel, who tried but failed to return it.

Marabel closed her eyes. *I wish*, she thought, deliberately using the forbidden term in case someone had given her a wish without telling her, *I wish that we find out how to get Marco home.*

Symposia tapped a page with a golden pointer, and one of the priests read the indicated passage aloud. The priests put their heads together and muttered to one another. It didn't take them long to settle on an interpretation. Marabel waited impatiently for the high priestess's translation. Symposia finally said in a low, lilting voice:

"*When the Chosen One recognizes himself, he shall prevail.*" She continued in her normal tone, "We have agreed that the Book declares that when Prince Marco regains his senses, he will be filled with power and knowledge. At that time, he will free himself from his captivity and vanquish Queen Mab—"

"She is not a queen!" King Matthew interrupted.

"—and then he will flee from her land and pass through the Impassable Forest and return home to Magikos, and Mab will lose her country."

"And what are we supposed to do until that happens?" King Matthew asked.

"We will wait," Symposia said.

"How long?"

"The Book doesn't specify a date," one of the priests said. "It doesn't have schedules. It just tells you what will happen. It assures us that Prince Marco will prevail, but it won't say when that will be."

King Matthew twirled his scepter, his brow furrowed in thought. Marabel anxiously bit her lip. Surely he'd order the guards out, perhaps even put on his royal armor and lead his troops on a rescue mission.

But the king didn't do either of those things. Instead, he said, "I'll send a messenger. I'll tell Mab, in no uncertain terms, that she is to release Marco and cease her demands. If she doesn't, we'll accept her declaration of war. There's nothing in the Book that would prevent me from sending such a message, is there?"

Marabel couldn't believe her ears. He was only going to send one lowly messenger when her brother's life was at stake? She whirled on her father. "*What?* We're not going to go after them and get him back? What if she tells that wizard to turn him into a snake before the messenger can get there? Or if Mab agrees to the war instead of letting him go? We have to get Marco *now*!"

"This is not for you to decide!" King Matthew barked, half rising from his throne and fixing Marabel with a furious glare. "We will do as Symposia advises!"

"But that's just wrong." Marabel fought to sound calm and failed. "The Book didn't say we couldn't help him."

Symposia interrupted the argument. "Your Majesty, this is a complicated question. It will take some time to find out if sending a messenger is in accordance with the dictates of the Book. We will start preparations for another Ritual of Consultation right away."

"What do you mean by 'some time'?" Queen Maggie asked. "I do hate the thought of our dear boy being held by that awful woman."

"We shall need only one day," the priestess answered.

"A whole day?" Marabel cried. "We only have a thrennight until she does something awful to him! And that's if she's telling the truth—her wizard might be turning Marco into something right now! Why can't we—"

Her father rose to his feet and pounded his scepter on the arm of his throne.

"Silence!" he said, and then he called, "Guard!" Lucius appeared at his side. "Take the princess to her chamber. Lock her in and bring me the key."

Marabel felt herself flush, embarrassed that the courtiers and guests had witnessed her being punished like a little girl. But she stood her ground and defiantly returned her father's glare.

"Dear, is this really necessary?" Queen Maggie asked. "Surely she doesn't need to be confined."

"She's so foolish she's liable to run out the front door and right into the dragon's mouth. No, she has to be locked in."

Marabel knew from experience that arguing would only make it worse. "It's all right," she told her stepmother. "I'll go." She'd let him think she was obeying, but she wouldn't give up. She'd find some way to rescue her brother.

But how?

Lucius led Marabel out of the banquet hall. She felt every eye on her. *I don't care*, she told herself, but Princess Ginevra's smirk made her cringe.

They passed the playroom where Marabel and Marco had spent most of their days before they'd had to "get serious," as their father said, and attend long, boring prince and princess lessons. The playroom door was open and Marabel caught a glimpse of their old favorite toys. Everything reminded her of Marco—the play castle that they had pretended to defend against toy dragons and ogres, the books about King Malcolm, an ancient set of wooden blocks that were chipped on their edges, the empty bowl that had once housed a talking goldfish that said nothing but "Food—food—food" until they liberated it into the moat.

Marabel's eyes smarted with tears. The fish was buried in the stable yard, the toy castle had fallen into disrepair, and now Marco was gone, too.

Lucius handed Marabel his handkerchief as he led her past the classroom. As she wiped away her tears, Marabel glimpsed the large map of the Desolate Barrens, the land governed by Mab. The map was illustrated with drawings of Evils: huge dragons, trolls with spiky clubs resting on their shoulders, hideous witches, animals dressed as people, and both kinds of faeries—the modern type, more properly called "fairies," who looked like human butterflies, and the sneaky faeries who looked like beautiful and friendly humans, but who beckoned travelers off the path and into their own shadowy realm. Was Marco already in that awful place?

Without warning, Lucius halted.

"What is it?" Marabel asked, frightened. "What's the matter, Lucius?"

He looked around. "We don't have much time," he whispered. "Someone might come by at any moment."

"Time for what?" Marabel tried to stay calm so she could grasp what Lucius was saying.

"I need to tell you what it is your aunt wants—why she kidnapped Marco. Your father won't speak of it—I think he's ashamed of how he behaved—and very few people know."

"What is it?" Marabel didn't know that she wanted to hear the answer, if it was something that made her father so ashamed he couldn't talk about it.

"Your aunt Mab was a remarkable girl. She was almost as good a fencer as you are. She's intelligent and strong-willed.

She would make a good ruler, in many ways. After your father became king, she tried to advise him on several occasions, and he finally lost his temper and told her to stop telling him what to do."

"I don't see why that would—" Marabel started, but Lucius interrupted her.

"Let me finish, Princess, please! She, too, lost her temper. She said that *she* should rule Magikos, instead of him. He accused her of treason. She said, 'You think that's treason? You haven't seen anything yet, brother dear!'"

"What happened?" Marabel asked.

"She tried to take Matthew's place on the throne. So your father banished her to the Barrens. He forbade anyone to talk about it." Lucius sighed. "He probably knows that he should have tried harder to reason with her, but you know how he is. Once he makes a decision, he can't bear to admit he was wrong."

"But what does this have to do with Marco?"

"Mab is going to hold him hostage until your father gives in to her demands. She—"

At that moment, a group of soldiers came down the hall. Lucius laid his finger on his lips, and they walked down the corridor in silence, with the guards so close behind them they couldn't talk again.

When Marabel and Lucius arrived at Marabel's chamber, Ellie was waiting. "Are you all right?" she asked Marabel anxiously.

"I'm fine, but you shouldn't be here," Marabel said. "Don't you know Lucius has to lock me in?" If a closed door upset Ellie, a locked one would throw her into a panic.

But Ellie seemed strangely calm about the prospect. "My mother told me always to stay by your side. Just like she was always by *your* mother's side."

Marabel squeezed Ellie's hand, and Ellie smiled at her.

Lucius started to speak, but just then a trumpet blast ripped through the air. "I have to go, Princess," he said. He laid a hand on Marabel's shoulder and looked her in the eyes. A little bit of the soreness around her heart lifted. He closed the door, and Marabel winced at the harsh sound of the key turning in the lock, followed by his retreating footsteps.

They were alone.

Marabel's chamber still smelled like hot water and soapweed, and her dirty red fencing garb still lay crumpled on the floor where she had left it—was it only a few hours ago? Hot tears rose to her eyes at the sight of the wooden practice sword, lying on her bed. Even in the excitement before the banquet, Marco had remembered to return it to her.

From outside came a deafening fluttering sound, and then shouts.

"What's happening?" Ellie cried.

They ran to the window. It was almost pitch-dark outside, but against the stars Marabel could make out the outline of a huge shape, moving swiftly. Its gigantic wings flapped noisily. "It's the dragon!" she said. "It's flying away!"

Then a motion from below caught Marabel's eye. It was a giant—probably the same one who had blocked her exit—and a group of other large beings. She couldn't make out much in the darkness, but they must be ogres and trolls, and who knew what else. They were all moving away from the palace, heading east toward the Impassable Forest, and the Wall, and the Desolate Barrens.

Mab must have sent word to her Evils to go home. This could only mean one thing: She was confident that she had gotten away. Marco was firmly in her grasp.

Marabel took a deep, shuddering breath and sat down, exhausted, on the small sofa. Ellie unclasped Marabel's bracelet and put it away, and then quietly set the room to order, picking up the dirty fencing garb, lining up the hairbrush and comb on the table, smoothing crumpled linens. These motions almost made it seem that today had been just an ordinary day.

Then Marabel realized that Ellie had stopped tidying and was standing at the door, her ear pressed to its crack.

"What are you listening to?" Marabel asked.

Ellie flapped a hand at her to shush. Slowly, silently, she reached into the pouch at her waist and pulled something out. She extended her open hand to Marabel, showing her what lay in her palm.

A key.

Marabel yelped, and then clapped a hand over her mouth.

Ellie's eyes flashed a warning. She said, a shade too loudly, "Sorry, Princess; I didn't mean to pull your hair. I'll brush more carefully."

Catching on, Marabel said, "It's all right, Ellie."

Ellie stepped closer and breathed in Marabel's ear, "I took the key from my mother's bureau."

"You *did*?" Marabel was astonished. Ellie was usually so obedient.

Looking both proud and a little scared of what she had done, Ellie laid a finger on her lips and nodded.

"So that's why you weren't afraid to be locked in," Marabel whispered back. "You knew you could get out."

Her mind raced at the thought of freeing herself and going to her father to convince him to send troops to rescue

Marco. But she knew it was hopeless. Never, ever would he go against the Book. That thought wouldn't even occur to him, or to any Magikian.

Except Marabel, it appeared, who was startled at the next thought that popped into her head.

Why not rescue Marco herself?

Ellie held up the key and looked at Marabel questioningly. "Go ahead," Marabel mouthed.

Ellie slid the key in the lock and turned it slowly. It protested with a squeak that made both girls wince.

"Wait a second," Marabel whispered. She took a bottle of perfumed oil from her dressing table and poured some into the lock. A lot dribbled out, but enough must have made it in; this time the key turned almost silently. Marabel eased the door open, took a cautious step, and peered down the hall. No guards. She went back into her chamber, leaving the door open a crack.

"Better?" she asked Ellie.

Ellie nodded.

"Good," Marabel said. "Because I need your help."

4

"No!" Ellie said after Marabel explained her plan. "I won't help you, because you're not going."

"Fine." Marabel yanked open a drawer and pulled out clothes, tossing them on the bed. "I'll just get ready by myself, then."

"Be serious." Ellie crossed her arms on her chest. "What can you do to help him? He's the Chosen One— the Book says he has to save himself."

"But even if he's the Chosen One, Aunt Mab's wizard can still turn him into a frog." Marabel didn't pause in her preparations. "And while we're sitting here waiting for Symposia to burn plants and jabber with the other priests, my aunt and my father could end up at war with each other. I want to save Marco, and I also need to save Magikos. It doesn't look like anyone else is going to do it!"

"If you leave, I'll tell someone," Ellie threatened.

"Go right ahead." Marabel wasn't worried. Ellie never tattled; she was always Marabel's ally. "This is what I have to do. My father's not going to go—he made that clear enough. He's never, ever questioned the Book. That's something he's proud of."

Marabel understood Ellie's shock; for a thousand years, the Magikians had followed the Book without question. It was hard to imagine not doing what it said.

"Something today made me think about that drought when we were little. Remember?" she asked.

Ellie nodded. "My father was worried about getting enough grain to feed the horses." Her father—dead two years now—had been the manager of the king's stable. "But what does that have to do with anything?"

"The Book never said there was going to be a drought—I guess because it wasn't a big enough problem to be worthy of mention. But it would have turned into a big problem if my father hadn't thought of a solution. A lot of people would have died. The Book didn't have to grant him permission to give away the royal grain. He just did it because he's the king and he has to do what's right for the whole country."

Ellie didn't answer.

"And those centaurs," Marabel added. "Remember? They could have caused a lot of trouble if they'd been allowed to run around much longer, but my father knew he could solve the problem by himself, since the Book didn't mention it."

"What are you saying?" Ellie sounded wary, even while her words posed a challenge to Marabel.

"My father's threatening to start a war if Marco doesn't come back. A war would *definitely* be in the Book, wouldn't it? So if the Book doesn't mention a war, that means it doesn't happen. And it means that something else has to happen instead to prevent it." She hoped Ellie could follow her; her own head was spinning and she wasn't sure if she'd explained clearly what she was thinking.

"So why doesn't it mention Marco being taken?" Ellie asked. "That's obviously something big, isn't it, to have the Chosen One kidnapped, even if there isn't a war? Shouldn't the Book talk about it?"

Marabel hesitated. This was a hard one. "I don't know,"

she finally admitted. "Maybe it's because he's going to escape and come home. Or maybe it's because someone will rescue him right away." Still, she knew the mere fact of the Chosen One being kidnapped was hugely important and *should* be mentioned in the Book. So why wasn't it? She'd have to think about it, and maybe ask Lucius. "Symposia says the Book is hard to understand sometimes," she said. "So maybe . . . maybe she's wrong about Marco having to save himself. Maybe it doesn't really say that."

Ellie wasn't convinced. "Maybe there's no war because your father's messenger is going to go to the Barrens and convince your aunt to give Marco back."

Marabel shook her head. "I don't believe that. Lucius says she's strong-willed, and she went to a lot of risk and trouble to get him. I don't believe she would just turn him loose because my father asked. And anyway, we can't risk it. There's only a thrennight until she turns Marco into a frog and then there's *sure* to be a war!"

"Let me get this straight," Ellie said. "You think you're actually doing what the Book says, and not going against it, by running away to rescue Marco?"

Was that what Marabel was saying? Did she understand the Book better than Symposia?

"I don't know," she admitted. "But I'm going anyway. I

can't just sit here." She went back to her packing. If she was going to do this, she had no time to waste.

Ellie watched in silence. Then she said, "We're going to need candles and some extra shoes."

Marabel was about to reach into her candle box when she realized what Ellie had said. "'We'?"

"My mother told me to—"

"Always stay by my side," Marabel finished for her.

"Besides," Ellie said resolutely, "Magikos is *my* home, too, and Marco is the twin brother of my best friend and my prince. If you're going, I'm going with you."

"Are you sure, Ellie?" Marabel asked. "It might be dangerous. It *will* be dangerous. We'll have to go through the Impassable Forest and into Mab's realm."

Ellie pretended not to hear the question, but her voice trembled a little as she said, "You'd better put on that old fencing garb. The new one is too special—someone might recognize you. I'll gather what we'll need. Do you have any money?"

Marabel shook her head. She had spent the little she had on a birthday gift for Marco. It was a dagger with a stone in the hilt that was supposed to keep the blade from getting dull. It must be on the table with all the other presents, still wrapped and waiting for him.

Then a greater challenge occurred to her. "Wait. How will we get past my father's troops? They must be guarding the walls. They'd be sure to see us."

"Leave that to me," Ellie said.

"What do you mean?"

Ellie drew close and whispered, "There's an escape tunnel that leads out of the palace grounds."

"There's a *what*? I don't believe you!"

Ellie nodded vigorously. "Its entrance is in the stable—my father showed it to me once. He said it was a secret passed down from parent to child for generations. He made me promise to keep it from everyone, even my mother, unless some terrible danger came to the royal family. I'd forgotten about it, but last night I had a dream that reminded me." Her forehead wrinkled. "It seemed strange, though—just when we need a secret way out, I dream about it."

It *was* strange, and it also seemed too good to be true. The dream couldn't be just chance. The thought gave Marabel new confidence. This rescue mission was meant to be!

While Marabel put on the red garb, Ellie spread two blankets on her bed and piled a change of clothes, a flask of water, a spare pair of boots, and a handful of candles onto each of them. She tied the corners together, making two neat packs. Marabel stuck the wooden sword into the belt around her tunic. It made her feel better.

Marabel itched to get started on their journey, but Ellie convinced her to wait. She pointed out that the more people there were around, the greater the risk they would run into someone. So Marabel watched impatiently out the window as exhausted guests climbed into their waiting coaches and rattled away.

Finally, no more coaches stood in the drive, and everything was silent indoors and out.

"Ready?" Marabel asked.

Ellie nodded. Each girl slung a pack over her shoulder, and they slipped out the door. Marabel closed and locked it, and slid the key into her pouch. She whispered, "If the door's locked, they might not check inside for a while. That'll give us some time."

They ran on tiptoe down the familiar corridor. *Will I ever see it again?* Marabel wondered. She felt an ache in the pit of her stomach. If only she could say good-bye to Malcolm and the little princesses! Would her father and stepmother worry about her? And would Lucius?

The palace was almost deserted due to the late hour. Marabel and Ellie had barely started down the longest corridor when the clanging footsteps of armored guards rang out not far from them. Marabel yanked Ellie into a store-room. They huddled together and hardly dared to breathe.

"Why, there you are, dear!"

Marabel whirled at the chirpy voice, sure they'd been caught. But it was only her old talking mirror.

"You look a *fright*! Don't think you're going anywhere looking like that! Ellie, what are you thinking? Fix your mistress's hair immediately, and wash her face and—"

The footsteps drew nearer. The guards would hear that silly mirror! In desperation, Marabel tossed a cloak over it. The voice continued, "—try to bring some color into her cheeks. . . ." and then faded into blessed silence as the foot-falls and voices progressed down the corridor. As soon as it seemed safe, Marabel and Ellie continued on their way.

Finally, they reached the empty kitchen. Coals still glowed in the hearth. The air was hot and stuffy with the smell of grease and onions and everything else that had gone into the dishes at the feast. Every surface was littered with vegetable peelings and bones and piles of flour. They hurriedly filled two sacks with as much food as they could carry.

Marabel opened the back door of the kitchen. The cool night air felt good on her hot cheeks. She located her favor-ite constellation—the Twins, who wheeled hand in hand across the sky in late summer and fall—and took a deep breath. "Come on," she said to Ellie.

As she hurried toward the stable, soft footfalls followed her. "Is the way out through the stable or behind it or what?" No reply. She turned around to see why Ellie hadn't answered.

But the footsteps weren't Ellie's. Instead, a large, oddly shaped form was silhouetted against the starry sky. As Marabel watched, stunned, it moved closer and reached out a misshapen limb in her direction. She tried to scream, but all that came from her throat was a dry croak.

Then the shape made a soft whickering sound, and Marabel realized what she was seeing. It was the long neck and head of her father's unicorn.

"Floriano," she exhaled with relief, and he stepped out of the shadows.

In the darkness, the unicorn looked gray. But he was really the royal colors of Magikos. In sunlight, Floriano shone pale blue, with a horn and hooves of such a brilliant gold that their glow made you squint. His white tail and mane were always twined with bright ribbons that streamed behind him when he cantered. But most amazingly, the black pupils of his golden eyes were perfect five-pointed stars.

Like all unicorns, Floriano loved girls, and he always followed Marabel around. It was sweet but it sometimes irritated her, especially since, whenever she sat down in his presence, he tried to lay his head on her lap. His horn had whacked her in the ribs more than once.

"What are you doing out of your stall?" Marabel asked, petting the unicorn's soft neck. He tossed his head and nosed her pack. "Sorry, no apple for you today. Go back to your stall and go to sleep. Someone will feed you in the morning."

Floriano snorted.

"Come on, Marabel," Ellie said, finally rounding the corner. "Let's go. Someone could see us."

Keeping close to the walls, they crept across the stable yard. Floriano followed them, as Marabel knew he would.

In the cozy stable, full of the warm smell of well-groomed horses and oats and leather, Marabel lit a candle. A snore came from the stall of her old black-and-white pony, and she heard soft breathing from the other animals. She tried to lead Floriano into his stall, but he stopped and tossed his head again.

"What's the matter?" Marabel stroked the unicorn's flank.

"Hurry," Ellie said. She cast an anxious glance back at the open stable door.

"I'm trying!" Marabel stepped into the unicorn's stall and shook the feed bucket. "Come *on*, Floriano. I don't have all night." He didn't move. "How did you get out anyway?"

"Leave him," Ellie said, impatient. "He'll be fine. It's going to start getting light soon." As if to confirm her words, the clock in the palace tower struck four.

"I can't," Marabel said. "If Floriano were to run away—" The unicorn stamped his hoof, narrowly missing Marabel's foot. "What *is* it? If only you could talk!"

"What makes you think I can't? You humans think you're the only ones with any brains!"

When Marabel realized that the unicorn had spoken, she asked in bewilderment, "You can *talk*?"

Ellie choked out, "It's some kind of enchantment! Marabel, we have to—"

"It's no enchantment," the unicorn said. "Well, in a way it is. Unicorns are magical beings, you know. And we can all talk."

"You *can*?" Marabel asked. "Why didn't you ever talk before?"

He blinked, his long lashes sweeping down on his cheek. "Maybe I didn't have anything to say."

"And what you had to say now is that you can talk?"

"Don't be stupid." His discourteous words sounded even

57

ruder coming from that beautiful face. "I have lot of things to say, actually. Like, what's with that groom with the cold hands? And what about the quality of the oats in here?"

At any other time, Marabel would have loved to talk with a unicorn. She was sure he would have much more interesting things to say than her old goldfish. But she was in a hurry. "I'll have someone check it out," she said. "Back in your stall, Floriano."

He tossed his head in a clear refusal. "No way. You're going somewhere exciting. I can tell. And I want to go with you." He reminded Marabel of her little sister Maisie, who was always trying to tag along after the twins.

"I mean it." Marabel tried to sound like her father. "Back in your stall *now*." Floriano cast her a bitter look but did as she said, dragging his golden hooves.

Marabel latched the stall securely, and the girls hurried into the tack room at the back of the stable. Ellie opened the door of a tall cabinet and pulled out scraps of leather, tools, buckles, balls of twine, and jars of leather polish. Marabel joined in, and together they heaped everything onto the floor.

"What are we doing?" Marabel asked.

"You'll see," Ellie said. She pulled out the now-empty shelves.

The inside of the cabinet looked how Marabel had expected—plain dark wood, with lighter horizontal stripes where the shelves used to be. Then she spotted a small, perfectly round hole at about waist height. Ellie poked her finger into it and tugged, and the entire piece of wood toppled out.

In the back of the cabinet, a wide hole now opened into a stone tunnel.

Marabel picked up her candle and peered in. Darkness swallowed the little light, and she could barely make out the long tunnel. It was tall and wide enough to allow a horse through. The tunnel sloped downward—to what, she couldn't see. Ancient black smudges on the walls and ceiling showed where torches had once burned. Faint marks of hooves in the deep dust told her that at some time, long ago, someone had ridden out this way.

"Where does it go?" Marabel asked, steeling her nerves.

"There's an opening at the edge of the royal woods, on the border of the Impassable Forest, I think."

The forest of Magikos ended at the Wall built by the great wizard Callum. On the other side of this ancient structure, the enchanted Impassable Forest of the Desolate Barrens began. Marabel hesitated, remembering tales of the Evils that lurked in Mab's dark woods. If a war started and Mab and her army could get through the Wall, Magikos would become full of Evils.

Then she thought of Marco, and of his limp arm as Mab and Veneficus carried him from the banquet hall, and her resolve firmed up. "It's now or never." Marabel stepped into the cabinet, but Ellie didn't move. "Come *on*, Ellie." Still nothing. She turned and saw Ellie hanging back.

"The tunnel's smaller than I remembered it," she said.

"Well, *you* were smaller when your father showed it to you, so it probably looked big to you then. But it's not really that small—see?" Marabel held the candle high to show that the ceiling was well above them. This was a mistake, because the light revealed a swarm of crickets and other small creatures that she didn't want to look at long enough to identify. She hastily lowered her arm.

Of course, even without the spiders and crickets, the tunnel must be frightening for someone with Ellie's fear of closed-off spaces. "You don't have to come if you're scared," Marabel said gently.

As Marabel expected, Ellie set her jaw. "I'm not any more scared than you are," she said. "You're not getting rid of me that easily!"

Marabel grinned to herself, and together they plunged into the darkness.

5

arabel started down the dark tunnel, followed
closely by Ellie.

The soft earth they were walking on muf-
fled their footfalls. Ellie breathed shallowly. Marabel
reached a hand behind her, and Ellie grasped it with
cold fingers. "It's okay," Marabel said. Her voice sounded
loud in the darkness.

They passed some round white rocks—no, they
weren't rocks. They were skulls. Marabel raised the
candle to cast them into shadow, and hurried her steps,
trying not to imagine how they had gotten there.

They walked a long way with only the dull thuds of their footsteps accompanying them. Then, from up ahead came a rumbling sound, and shouts, and voices singing. Maybe it was the little men who lived in tunnels underground. Some of them were friendly, she'd always heard, but some . . .

Marabel stumbled against something, nearly dropping the candle. Ellie bumped into her from behind. "What are you stopping for?" she hissed.

Marabel lowered the candle and saw, to her surprise, that she had stubbed her toe against the bottom step of a flight of stairs.

"This must be the way out," she whispered. "See?" She raised the candle to reveal that a piece of the ceiling was made of wood. She made out a hinge on one side of the board. "This must be a door." She snuffed out the candle, and Ellie gave a little squawk.

"We can't risk anyone seeing a light when we open it. It must still be dark outside," Marabel explained. "You're fine. We'll be out in the open in a minute." She hoped she sounded calmer than she felt. She was more excited than frightened—this was the real start of their quest to rescue Marco!

Marabel felt her way up the stairs, the stone steps cold beneath her hands. She shivered as something with lots of tiny legs skittered over her fingers. One, two . . . she counted to thirteen before she bumped her head on something. "Ow!" escaped her lips.

The sound of music continued, and now Marabel could tell that it was coming from above them, not deep in the earth. It was the Magikian anthem.

Ellie crept up next to her. "I have to get out," she panted. "*Right now.*"

"Ellie, I don't know how—" was all Marabel could manage before Ellie shoved hard against the wooden ceiling that Marabel had hit her head on, making it shift a little.

"Let me help," Marabel said. She planted her feet firmly and set her back against the board. "One, two, three!" she urged, and with all her might she strained and Ellie pushed, and the door flew open so suddenly that they lost their footing and tumbled back down to the bottom of the stairs.

Above them, the trapdoor gaped open, and Marabel shuddered as she imagined a helmeted head appearing, a soldier catching sight of a runaway princess and her maid. But all she saw were clouds streaked with the pink and orange of the rising sun.

Marabel climbed back up the steep steps and cautiously looked around. The trapdoor had been covered in a few inches of dirt and grass, making it invisible when closed.

But there was still one huge problem: They now were in the royal garden and not in the forest, as Ellie had told her they would be. This meant they could easily be seen by sentries patrolling the palace walls.

"What on earth is the point of a tunnel that doesn't take you all the way to a safe place?" Ellie asked.

"It must have been built a long time ago," Marabel said. She pressed her fingers to her temples, trying to remember the boring lessons on family history that she and Marco had mostly ignored. "The royal gardens," she said, "are where there used to be a wild forest. When the tunnel was built, this opening must have been in the middle of that forest." The woods lay only a few hundred yards away—an easy walk, normally, but tonight the shelter of the trees seemed frighteningly distant.

Then a voice behind them said, "Hey!"

Both girls let out a yelp and leaped into each other's arms, trembling.

"Where did that come from?" Marabel asked, looking around.

"Down here!" came from inside the tunnel.

"It's Floriano again!" Ellie said in disbelief.

"What are you doing here?" Marabel cried down the hatchway, relieved and annoyed at the same time.

"It's *boring* in the stable," he said. "It's just ponies and horses and a stupid donkey, and they don't care about anything except eating hay and oats and snoozing in the sun. Unicorns aren't supposed to get fat and take naps. If you're going on an adventure, I want to go with you."

"This isn't just an adventure," Marabel said. "It's a rescue mission. And how did you get out of your stall?" She knew she had latched it tight.

"We have our ways," Floriano said vaguely.

"We who?" Marabel asked.

"What does it matter?" Ellie broke in. "The guards could see us at any second. We have to go—now!"

"Where are you going anyway?" the unicorn asked. "It might not be worth my time to go with you."

"My brother was kidnapped," Marabel said. "We're going to rescue him."

"Oh, that does sound adventurous!" Floriano said. "Count me in."

"No way," Ellie said. "You'd make us too visible."

Floriano cocked his head toward the soldiers marching along the walls. "How were you planning to get past *them*?"

"We're still working on that," Marabel said, although she hadn't come up with any ideas yet.

"I'll take care of it." Floriano sounded smug. "I'm going

to distract them. As soon as you hear me whinny like a horse, run as fast as you can toward the forest."

Before they could answer, Floriano clambered up the stairs and positioned himself in front of the palace walls. His white mane and tail fluttered in the breeze, and his horn and hooves glinted in the growing light. He looked magnificent as he arched his neck and pawed the ground. He raised his head proudly, clearly expecting to hear gasps and murmurs from the awestruck soldiers.

But none came. Floriano lifted a golden hoof and coughed. Not a single head turned in his direction. Despite the danger of their situation, Marabel had to press a hand over her mouth to stifle a giggle.

Floriano stamped furiously. He reared, his golden hooves pawing the air. He was truly a splendid sight, and finally someone saw him. A soldier called out, "The king's unicorn!" and someone else yelled, "Seize him before he escapes! The king will pay a great reward!" and then lots of soldiers shouted and ran in his direction.

Floriano gave a leap and galloped away, drawing the soldiers after him. After a moment, his whinny rose over the commotion.

"Now!" Marabel grabbed Ellie's hand and they fled toward the trees.

It felt like forever before they reached darkness of the forest. At last they plunge breath ragged and their sides aching.

The girls ran until their breath and strength gave out. They collapsed and sprawled, gasping, on the dead leaves and pine needles. After a moment, they pushed themselves up to sitting, letting their packs slip off their backs.

Ellie wiped a strand of hair off her face. "Phew," she said. "Now what?"

"We need to go deeper into the trees," Marabel said.

The problem with that was that it would make it harder for Floriano to find them. But what choice did they have? They had to hurry to rescue Marco in time. The Barrens were vast, and there were mountains and rivers and who knew what else between them and Mab's castle. It would take every minute of the thrennight to get there in time—if that was even enough.

They shouldered their packs and picked their way over roots and fallen branches. They couldn't find a path, so their progress was agonizingly slow as they pushed through bushes and brambles. Gradually, the sight and sounds of the palace faded.

Behind them, the ground shook with the pounding of hooves. Before they could hide, Floriano burst through the ᴬnches and cantered up to them. "So which way are we going?" he asked brightly.

Marabel sighed, resigned. She couldn't force the unicorn to return to his stall, and he obviously wasn't going there voluntarily. She looked at Ellie, who shrugged.

"All right," Marabel said reluctantly. "You can come."

"Hooray!" Floriano pranced in place. "We're going on an adventure!"

Marabel hoped he was right. At the moment, rescuing her brother felt more like a big mistake than a grand adventure.

At first, their adventure was remarkably unadventurous. Marabel looked for the rising sun so she could lead the way toward the east, but the trees were so thick that she couldn't see the sky very well. When she finally got her bearings, they used a trick Lucius had taught her: to go straight, find two landmarks in a line, and when you get to the first, line up the second one with a new one. The three travelers took turns being in front, since it was tiring to push through branches and find footing among the fallen leaves and rotten sticks.

For a while they walked along a stream. Its water tinkled hypnotically, making Marabel's eyelids droop. After a few miles, Floriano asked, "So which way are we going?"

"East, to the Wall," Marabel answered shortly. She was so tired from staying up all night that she could hardly talk.

"What wall?" the unicorn asked.

Ellie and Marabel stopped and stared at Floriano. Unconcerned, he stopped, too, and ripped up a mouthful of grass.

"Are you *serious*?" Ellie asked. "You don't know about the Wall?"

Floriano shook his elegant head and swallowed. "I told you, those horses and that stupid donkey aren't interested in anything but food and sleep. If they ever talked about a wall, I didn't hear them. Why are we going to a wall?"

Right now, food and sleep sounded too appealing to Marabel. They'd been traveling for hours, but they didn't have time for a nap or a snack. "Let's sit down and rest a minute while I tell you," she suggested. They wouldn't be any good to Marco if they exhausted themselves in the first few hours of their journey.

They drank their fill from the stream and then settled into the shade of a tall tree, Floriano folding his long legs under him like a big blue dog. Ellie took some bread and cheese out of her pack and, between swallows, Marabel told Floriano the history of the Wall.

"One thousand years ago, Magikos was a wild land where Evils ran free, until—"

"'Evils'?" the unicorn interrupted. "What are 'Evils'?"

"Magical beings," Ellie said. "You know, elves and giants and ogres and uni—" She stopped abruptly.

"Uni-what?" Floriano asked suspiciously. "Universities? Uniforms?" Ellie's face showed deep embarrassment. "Unicycles?"

"Oh, be quiet, Floriano," Marabel said. "You know what she meant. *Wild* magical beings. Not tame ones like you."

Floriano rose to his hooves, his nostrils flaring. "So I'm a tame unicorn, am I? Domesticated? Is that what you think of me?"

Marabel sighed. "Do you want to hear about the Wall or don't you?"

Floriano didn't answer, so Marabel went on. "Anyway, my ancestor, King Manfred, defeated the Ev—um, defeated the *enemy*—and sent them to the Desolate Barrens in the eastern part of the country. A few humans went with them, but most stayed in Magikos. Manfred's wizard, Callum, built a great Wall dividing the two parts of the kingdom, weaving magic and stones together so that none of the—so that no one could go through it. When my aunt Mab was banished to the Barrens, she proclaimed it a separate land, and said she was its queen."

"She isn't, though," Ellie put in. "The Desolate Barrens are still part of Magikos."

"So do you mean to tell me," Floriano said, still sounding huffy, "that there are more unicorns on the other side of this wall we're going to?"

"I expect so," Marabel replied. "Along with lots of other . . . things."

"Well, let's go, then." Floriano stamped a slender hoof.

Marabel turned slowly, trying to catch a glimpse of the afternoon sun, and saw a small spot of light through the branches. But the light was purplish, not like sunlight, and it glimmered and even seemed to move from branch to branch. *Some kind of firefly*, Marabel thought, although she had never heard of a purple firefly before.

The light settled on a branch right in front of her. She leaned in cautiously so as not to frighten it away.

Marabel caught her breath. What she was looking at was undeniably a fairy, one of the tiny, winged sort, not the kind that lured people into their realm. It wore a long purple robe, and its face, hands, and bare feet glowed so much that it was hard to see its features. Light spilled out from under its flowing robe and through the ends of the sleeves and the collar.

"Oh!" Ellie breathed in Marabel's ear.

Floriano stretched his neck forward like a cat, his nostrils twitching.

The little being said something, but its voice was so tiny that Marabel had to lean in, holding her hood back, in order to hear it. "What did you say?" she asked.

She couldn't be sure, but it sounded like the fairy kept repeating, "Pay attention! Use your eyes!"

Marabel looked around, but didn't see what the fairy was talking about—not that she could see much of anything in the dark woods. She was about to question the fairy again, but it flew away, zigging and zagging through the trees, rapidly disappearing from sight.

"What now?" Ellie asked.

Marabel looked in the direction that the fairy had flown and spotted a patch of trees off to one side. They looked a little different from the rest. Strangely, the tree trunks seemed flat, not round.

"Let's try over there," Marabel suggested. She fought her way through a particularly prickly shrub, and when she finally looked up, she realized that what she had thought were flat trees were actually wooden boards. She was staring at a huge door.

Big metal hinges ran up one side of it, but there was no doorknob or handle of any kind. It was much bigger than any door she had ever seen, even counting the enormous one leading out of the royal palace to the drawbridge. And it stood all by itself, surrounded by trees and bushes. On either side of it, sunlight was filtering through leaves, and an occasional squirrel scrambled up a trunk. It looked like a perfectly ordinary part of the forest, except for the gigantic door standing in the midst of everything.

Ellie stopped short just behind Marabel. "What in Book's name is a door doing in the middle of the woods?"

"Someone's idea of a joke," Marabel said. "Why would anyone go to the trouble of going through a door when you could just go around it?" She started to walk past the door, but immediately slammed into something invisible and staggered back, rubbing her nose where she had banged it.

At that instant, a green light flashed, and where before there had been nothing, now they faced a gigantic stone wall that stretched out of sight in both directions. It was taller than three men standing on one another's shoulders.

"The Wall!" Marabel exclaimed. "It must have an invisibility spell on it that gets broken when someone touches it."

She ran a tentative finger along the rough stone, covered in moss and lichen, marveling at the massive blocks and their ancient majesty.

"Do you think we can open it?" Ellie asked.

The enormous wooden door was remarkably sound for something exposed to wind and rain and sun, and its hinges—each one bigger than both of Marabel's hands together—were made of a black metal that didn't show a single spot of rust. That was a sure sign of magic. But even after the green flash, she still couldn't see a handle, a key-hole, or even a door knocker.

"There must be a way," Marabel said. "What's the point of a door you can't open?"

"Let's push it," Ellie suggested. The girls put all their strength into shoving, but the door didn't budge. They tried working their fingers into the cracks between the boards to give it a pull, but they couldn't get a grip. Briefly, Marabel considered trying to climb over the Wall, but it was much too high.

They sprawled, exhausted, on the ground. "What do we do now?" Ellie asked.

"We have to look for another way to get past the Wall," Marabel said. "There *must* be another opening. Mab had to get through somehow." She sat up. "Oh!"

"What?" Ellie asked.

"Don't you see?" Marabel pointed around them. "See those footprints? Someone must have been here recently. And look—scorch marks! I bet that dragon made them. This door *must* be the way Mab came through with her wizard."

"So what?" Ellie asked. "We still can't open it. We've tried everything."

Floriano cleared his throat. "Not quite everything."

"What do you mean?" Despite being tired and hungry and worried and discouraged, Marabel tried not to snap at Floriano. It wasn't his fault that the rescue mission was failing. She was the leader, so it was *her* fault.

"Oh, I don't know," he said airily. "I thought I might be able to do something, but maybe you don't want an *Evil* to help you."

"Oh, stop it," Ellie said. "You know I didn't mean you."

Floriano went on as though he hadn't heard her. "I don't blame you, though. If you had a *real* unicorn with you, one who still had magic in his horn . . ." At the last word, his horn glimmered faintly. "Magic specifically for opening locks and undoing locking spells . . ." The glimmer brightened to a glow.

Marabel wasn't sure she understood. "So unicorns have a way to open doors and gates and things?"

Floriano didn't answer and he made no move toward the door, but his horn now shone like the reflection of the sun on a pond.

Marabel sighed, pretending she didn't really care. "I guess you've forgotten how to do it," she said. "Oh well. All those years of living in a stable with that donkey must have tamed all the magic right out of you."

Floriano's horn suddenly blazed so bright that the girls had to squint. With a great whinny, the unicorn reared up on his hind legs, his horn flashing and throwing off sparks. He pawed the air with his hooves, and as he dropped down to all fours again, he allowed the tip of his horn to graze the edge of the huge door.

It sprang open as though blown by a mighty wind.

Silence hung in the air. The girls stared through the opening, their mouths wide open. Floriano's sides heaved with the effort to catch his breath.

"So that's how you got out of your stall!" Marabel exclaimed.

Floriano tossed his head. His horn, while still a lovely gold, no longer glowed. "It's a skill we've developed, we unicorns. People are always trying to trap us, you know. They lure us into gardens, where we lay our heads on girls' laps. We love to do that. The girls always pet us and feed us delicious snacks. But then it turns out that the gardens have fences around them, and someone closes the gate, and then . . . there we are. Prisoners."

Marabel realized she'd never known where Floriano had come from—whether he'd been born in captivity, or if he'd been taken from one of the few herds of wild unicorns that people still occasionally glimpsed in Magikos. "Did someone capture you like that?"

Floriano snorted. "If it was that easy to capture unicorns, there'd be hundreds of us in zoos and in people's stables, sharing stalls with stupid donkeys. Capture happens only once every hundred years or so. No, my ancestors were trapped many years ago. My family has lived with humans for generations."

"Why didn't you say something about this earlier?" Ellie asked. "Was it fun for you to watch us trying, knowing you could just touch the door with your horn and it would open?"

"A little," Floriano admitted. "But mostly, I . . . Well, I wasn't sure it would work on this particular door. I mean, if there are unicorns on the other side of the Wall, over there"—he nodded at the forest they could see through the open door—"why didn't your aunt use them to open it a long time ago? Why did she wait until now to steal your brother?"

"I don't know," Marabel said. "But we're wasting time. Let's go on, and we can try to figure it out later. We only have twelve days left."

"You first," Floriano said, and Marabel, feigning courage, stepped through the open door, followed by Ellie and then the unicorn.

They turned and watched the Wall fade away.

Her entire life, Marabel had heard how frightening and dangerous the Barrens were. The land was lawless, everyone said, and full of Evils waiting to pounce on Magikians who somehow found their way in.

Instead, this place looked and sounded a lot like home. Leaves rustled in the wind the same way they did on the Magikian side, the trees looked the same, and the rays of sun that made it through the dense leaves had the same colorless light as at home.

Marabel couldn't help feeling disappointed. *This* was what she had been afraid of all her life? This ordinary forest?

"We must still be in Magikos," Ellie said.

But then a bear came trundling past them, wearing a flowered hat. She nodded politely at the group and said,

"Nice day, isn't it?" in a snuffly kind of voice, and was gone before they could answer. They watched her disappear in stunned silence.

Marabel said, "Ellie, I don't think we're in Magikos anymore."

6

hich way now?" Floriano asked.

Marabel gathered her wits and con-
jured up in her imagination the big map
that hung on the wall of the palace classroom. "There
should be a path that runs near the Wall," she said. "Let's
find it and see if we come across someone who can give
us directions to Mab's castle."

They walked and walked, but the path, if it was still
there—for the map in the classroom was at least as old
as King Matthew, and paths quickly become overgrown
if nobody walks on them—proved impossible to find.

To Marabel's disappointment, they didn't pass any more magical beings.

The wind picked up and it started to rain. They walked hunched over in a vain attempt to keep at least a little dry.

And then came a sound that they didn't expect. It was a cough. Ellie, who was in the lead, nearly bumped into a man dressed like a farmer or a woodcutter, who was leaning against a tree. She jumped back, but he smiled at them in a friendly manner, his shining teeth visible through his beard.

Marabel said, "Good evening," as civilly as she could manage.

"Nasty weather," he said. Marabel and Ellie murmured in agreement. Floriano hung back. He pawed the ground nervously and sniffed the air.

"Where are you going in the rain?" the man asked.

Ellie leaned in close to Marabel and murmured, "Something's not right. Look at Floriano. Let's not let this guy know where we're heading."

Marabel swallowed. Floriano did look agitated. What was bothering him? So she followed Ellie's suggestion. "We're going to my grandmother's house," was all she could think of. "We didn't know it was going to rain."

"A little late in the day to be visiting, surely."

"She's sick," Ellie put in. "We're taking food and blankets to her." She shifted her pack on her shoulders.

"How nice." He still didn't let them pass. "I wonder if you three could help me with something I found?"

Marabel was caught off-guard by the question. She asked eagerly, "Is it a boy? We're looking for a boy, one about our age." She ignored the sharp nudge of Ellie's elbow.

The man nodded. "Yes, it's a boy. He's terribly wounded."

"Marco!" Marabel cried. Could he have escaped their aunt? Was that how he got hurt?

He nodded again. "Yes, that was the name. And he said two girls and a unicorn were wandering around in the forest, and they would help him."

For a moment Marabel's heart thudded eagerly, but something was not right. How would Marco know that she and Ellie were looking for him, much less Floriano?

Actually, the man hadn't said he'd found a boy. She was the one who had said it. The man had just agreed.

Marabel muttered to Ellie, "Let me try something. Play along." Turning to the man, she tried to smile. "Thank you, sir. I hope he's not too badly hurt. Our—our bull gored him yesterday."

"Yes, that's what he said. He ran away from the bull and got lost in the woods."

"I'm surprised you could see him in the rain, what with his black hair," Ellie said.

The man asked impatiently, "Do you want to stand here chatting, or do you want to help your friend?"

The clouds thinned a little, finally allowing some sunshine through, and Marabel could make out the man's face more clearly. She realized that he didn't only have a beard.

His whole face was covered in bristly fur.

And he had a pointy muzzle-like nose, and his eyes were red.

At Marabel's horrified gasp, the stranger bared his teeth in a snarl. Two long, sharp fangs gleamed from the corners of his mouth. *An Evil!*

Ellie screamed and Floriano whinnied. Without thinking, Marabel yanked the wooden sword from her belt and whacked the man-wolf over the head. He howled an inhuman sound.

"Run!" Marabel shouted, and the two girls took off through the trees. The Evil snarled and sprang after them. Marabel felt herself being yanked backward—he had grabbed her pack! She desperately shrugged it off, stumbling over rocks and branches.

Marabel glanced back to see Floriano whirl around and kick the man-wolf so hard that he flew through the air and slammed into a tree. He howled again, but then scrambled to his feet and lunged at the unicorn. Marabel tore her eyes away from them and sped through the trees, catching up with Ellie. Floriano galloped past them, shouting, "Run! Run! Run!" Marabel didn't have the breath to say, "What does it *look* like we're doing?"

She just ran.

Marabel thought her legs and lungs would give out, when Ellie slipped and crashed down, her arms flailing. Marabel leaped over her, turned back, and hauled Ellie to her feet. But Ellie let out a cry and crumpled to the ground.

"My ankle," she said. "I think I've twisted it."

Floriano cantered back and looked down at Ellie, water dripping off his horn. He raised his head, and his large nostrils sniffed the air. "We can stop now. The beast is gone," he said. "I *knew* there was something wrong about him. He didn't smell right."

"Are you sure he's gone?" Marabel asked.

The unicorn nodded. "He can't catch up. Those beasts are fast, but they don't have much stamina. Not like unicorns."

Marabel allowed herself to relax a little and caught her breath.

Ellie flexed her ankle and winced. "Can you walk?" Marabel asked her.

Ellie shook her head. Marabel glanced at Floriano.

"What?" he asked. She nodded at Ellie. "Oh," he said. "I suppose you want me to carry her. I'm a unicorn, you know, not just a horse with a horn. I'm a *magical being*."

Ellie rubbed her ankle and gave a little moan.

Floriano looked down at her again, and his expression softened. He gave an exaggerated sigh. "All *right*, if I have to. But I won't be able to go fast with her on me—or very far, either. We'll have to find shelter soon." Marabel helped Ellie onto the unicorn's back and they set off again, Floriano's hooves slipping in the mud.

The rain went on for hours, and they had to stop to rest more and more often. Marabel realized that Ellie's pack must have slipped off, too. It was too late to go back for either of them. For all she knew, the man-wolf was waiting for them.

They walked and walked, with Marabel in front. She was hungry, and from the squeaks and grumbles that came from her friend's stomach, Ellie was, too.

Even the few birds still singing in the trees sounded glum.

More clouds rolled in, until darkness enveloped them and thunder rumbled ever closer. It was raining so hard that the drops came through the thick leaves and soaked them. They couldn't see more than a few feet ahead, and Floriano's hooves and Marabel's feet kept slipping. Marabel despaired of finding even a dry spot under a tree, much less a cottage.

Then the sound of Floriano's hooves changed, making an echo, and the rain ceased abruptly.

"Ellie!" Marabel cried. "Floriano! We're in a cave!"

Of course, Ellie panicked at the word *cave*. She slid off Floriano's back. Marabel grabbed Ellie's sleeve as she tried to hobble back outside.

"We have to stay here for now," Marabel said firmly. "It's dry, and we're out of the wind. You can sit right by the entrance so you won't feel closed in." It took a little coaxing, but Ellie eventually agreed.

Marabel made a cautious circuit of the cave. It was enormous—she couldn't see the ceiling in the dim light—but it had only one opening. The cave was dry and the floor wasn't too rough. It could have been much, much worse.

She knew it was probably a lot worse wherever Marco was. From the little Marabel had heard about her aunt, Mab wasn't exactly kind. She wouldn't treat a hostage well, especially if she was planning to turn him into a frog or a snake. What if Marabel rescued her brother too late, condemning him to live in a terrarium and eat flies for the rest of his life?

Marabel couldn't stop the tears from running down her cheeks, and was grateful that the light was too weak to show them. She didn't want to worry Ellie. But when a sob burst from her throat, Ellie came over and wrapped her arms around her. She didn't say anything, but she didn't need to.

They sat in miserable silence for a long time before Ellie said, "We have to go back."

Marabel sat up. "We can't abandon Marco!"

"We have no food," Ellie pointed out. "No food and no candles, and no money to buy them with even if we find a village. We nearly got eaten by a man-wolf. My ankle's getting better"—she stuck out her leg and twirled her foot, wincing only a little—"but what if I'd broken it? Floriano couldn't carry me the whole way to your aunt's castle."

Floriano raised his elegant head. "Go back? Why didn't you think of that earlier, before we got soaked and starved and—"

"But think how much worse it must be for Marco!" Marabel said.

"We don't know what we're doing!" Ellie shot back. "I shouldn't have let you convince me. I should have gone right to your father and told him what you were planning!"

"Ellie's right," Floriano said. "I wanted an adventure. This isn't an adventure. It's a mistake. Let's go home."

"You can do what you want," Marabel said. "Go home. Fine with me. I'll go on by myself. I can't leave my brother."

"But if Floriano and I go back without you," Ellie said,

"we'll get in terrible trouble. They'll be angry at us for abandoning you. If you go, I have to go with you. I have to stay by your side, remember?"

"I don't think your mother would have said that if she knew someday we'd be running away," Marabel said. "She was only telling you to stay near me so you could be helpful."

Ellie didn't answer as she lay down on the ground and crossed her arms. "If you don't want me here, Marabel, you can just say so." Without waiting for an answer, she turned on her side, her back toward Marabel, and went to sleep.

Marabel lay awake for a long time and listened to the others breathing. She felt bad that she'd hurt Ellie's feelings, but this journey to save Marco was the most important thing she'd ever done. Why couldn't her best friend understand that?

If they really want to go back, I'll walk a little way toward home with them, she told herself, *and then I'll find some cottager or charcoal burner or someone who will help them the rest of the way, and I'll come back and continue on to Aunt Mab's.* Without food? Without supplies? And could she arrive before her father's messenger? Her mind whirled until she fell asleep.

She had nightmares of Marco imprisoned in a hideous

cell, reaching through the bars and calling out to her to save him. Then she dreamed that the cave walls around her were shaking and twisting and turning, threatening to collapse and crush her with jagged boulders.

Her eyes popped open. A little light was coming into the cave. Ellie and Floriano were still asleep and breathing peacefully. The only other sounds were early-morning bird-calls and the wind in the leaves. In the dim light, the cave revealed itself to be even larger than she had thought. Its walls were ordinary stone and dirt, not the crushing boulders she had seen in her nightmare.

Floriano opened his eyes, his long lashes sweeping up to reveal his star-shaped pupils. He glanced at Marabel, yawned, and hoisted himself to his feet, remarking, "I don't suppose there's anything for breakfast."

A strangled sound from Ellie saved her from having to answer. Ellie scrambled to her feet and ran out the narrow cleft to the open air, limping only a little. "I want to go," she said over her shoulder, keeping her eyes averted from the cave.

Marabel and Floriano joined Ellie in the thick woods. The sun finally came out all the way, and the light filtering through the dense leaves cast a green glow on the ground.

Marabel looked around. "This is the way we came," she said. "Come on. I'll go partway back with you, and we'll find someone to help you the rest of the way. You can tell my parents that I made you go back, and they won't punish you for leaving me."

Unexpectedly, Ellie said, "No."

"No?" Marabel asked.

Ellie thrust her chin out. "I woke in the night and thought about it. Then a little voice in my head reminded me that I'm a Magikian. That a woman came and kidnapped our prince. As long as I don't have to sleep in a cave again, I'm with you."

Floriano heaved an exasperated sigh and said, "I'm not going to let anyone say that the unicorn was the one who gave up while two humans risked their lives on an adventure. Count me in, too."

Marabel was so moved, she found it hard to speak. "I'm not your princess out here. If we're going to do this, we'll do it together, all right?"

They nodded. "And, Mara," Ellie said, "I'm sorry about what I said. You're my friend, and I—"

"I know," Marabel said. "Me too."

They turned east. Ellie was walking much better now, so the three of them once again took turns being in the lead. Marabel was in front, thinking that they'd be wandering in this wet, chilly forest forever, when a squirrel chittered at them. She glanced in its direction and caught a glimpse of something white. It was small—about her height—and it didn't move. It was unnaturally straight in this place of twisted branches and crooked tree trunks. Floriano caught sight of it, too, and called out, "Hey! What's that?"

Marabel reached it first. She touched it tentatively. It was a board with black letters on it.

"What is it?" Floriano asked again.

"A signpost," Marabel said. "See?" The arrow on her side of the post said GIANTS' LAIR, TWO DAYS' JOURNEY. No way they were going in *that* direction!

"Look," Floriano said. On the other side were two signs pointing different ways. "What do they say?"

Ellie read aloud, "Castle by bridge, one thousand five hundred pebbles." And the other, "Castle by boat, three thousand four hundred pebbles."

"Pebbles?" Marabel asked.

"A payment?" Ellie guessed. "We don't have any money, but we could easily pick up some pebbles."

"More than three thousand of them?" Floriano asked.

"Whatever it means," Marabel said, "the bridge looks like a better way to go."

"I'm not getting in any boat anyway," Floriano said. "I don't think I could. We unicorns aren't built for such things."

They followed the sign pointing toward the bridge and emerged from the forest at the base of a tall hill. A low rushing sound grew louder as they walked, until it became a continuous roar. Surely they hadn't mistaken what the sign said—surely they weren't about to arrive at a lair full of roaring giants?

They rounded a curve and came to a long, steep gorge. A river foamed at the bottom, tumbling over sharp rocks and broken tree limbs. It looked dangerous, but at least it wasn't giants.

And fortunately, the bridge was only a short distance away. It looked sturdy, with broad wooden planks held up by a large stone support.

Marabel's heart rose. They were out of the woods, and it was a beautiful day, and the bridge was large and strong. At this rate, they'd be at Mab's castle in no time!

She caught sight of another sign. This one hung above the bridge, with letters written on it so crudely that they were hard to read. As she tried to decipher it, she nearly plowed into Ellie, who had stopped short.

"What is it?" Marabel asked, but then she saw it, too, and it felt like a cloud had covered the sun, so dark did the world become.

It looked like—yes, it was a troll.

7

ow Marabel could make out the sign hanging above the bridge: STOP! PAY TROLL. A crooked arrow pointed to the left at the words EXACT CHANGE and another arrow went to the right, where the sign said ATTENDANT.

The troll was sitting on a stump under the second sign, with his feet propped up on a rock. He was as ugly as trolls were always said to be, with wisps of olive-green hair scattered over his lumpy head, a warty nose, and tiny eyes. He wore a dark blue shirt and matching trousers, like a uniform. The pants stopped right below his knees, showing his crooked ankles and bare, bumpy feet. He held something in one knobby hand.

"He hasn't seen us," Marabel whispered to Ellie. "Let's get out of here."

Before Ellie could answer, the troll rose to his feet and looked straight at them. Ellie squeaked and buried her face in Marabel's shoulder. Marabel tried to say something, but her mouth just opened and shut silently. Floriano whickered nervously.

"Oh, hey," the troll said.

If this wasn't the last thing Marabel expected a bridge troll to say, it was way down on the list. Why not something more trollish, like, "Who dares try to cross my bridge?"

She swallowed her terror and said, "Hey."

"You can't believe how long I've been waiting for someone to come by." The troll broke out in a brown-toothed grin that didn't do much to improve his looks. "Now pay up."

Marabel shook her head. "We don't have any gold."

The troll's face wrinkled hideously in disappointment. "Precious stones?" She shook her head again. "Silk or velvet?" Once again, Marabel had to disappoint him.

"There's just one thing left, then." The troll took a step toward them and the girls clung together, Floriano trying unsuccessfully to hide behind them. Was the troll going to eat them one at a time, or all at once? Marabel wondered in horror.

"You have to answer three questions," he said. "If you do, I'll let you cross."

They looked at one another. "Let's try," Ellie said. "What do we have to lose? If we can't answer him, surely there's another bridge somewhere, maybe one without a troll."

"All right," Marabel said, and she turned to the troll. "We accept."

"And of course," the troll went on, "if you can't answer, I have to throw you off the bridge." They looked down at the jagged rocks and rushing water and then back at the troll. He shrugged apologetically. "Sorry, but those are the rules." He tapped the leather-bound book he was holding. The gold writing on the cover read, *Rules and Regulations Governing the Crossing of Bridges, Causeways, Dams, and Dikes: A Practical Guide for the Guardian Troll.*

"Ready for your first question?" he asked brightly, as though this were a game.

"Wait a minute," Marabel said. "Just wait. You tricked us. You didn't tell us everything before we agreed, so forget it. No questions, no throwing anybody off any bridge. Come on, Ellie." But the troll let out an angry shout, and immediately their way was blocked by three more trolls, each bigger and uglier than the last. They all wore the same dark blue uniform.

"That will teach you," said the biggest and ugliest troll, "not to agree to anything unless you know what's in the small print, so to speak. Rules are rules. It's a good lesson to learn."

"Not that they'll get a chance to profit from the lesson!" said a scrawny violet troll, and all three burst out laughing.

The bridge troll looked embarrassed. "Those are my supervisors," he said.

The supervisors growled at Marabel and arranged themselves in a line across the bridge.

Marabel looked at the trolls and realized that they didn't have any choice except to answer the questions. Marabel straightened and took a deep breath. Lucius always said this was the best way to calm yourself. "So ask us your three questions," she said as bravely as she could.

"No," the troll said. "Three questions each!"

"Sorry." Marabel mimicked his gruff tone. "That will teach you not to agree to anything unless you know everything about it. You were looking at all of us when you said, 'You have to answer three questions.' That means three questions *all together*. So what's the first one?"

The troll, looking unhappy, glanced at his supervisors.

The violet one said, "She's right, I'm afraid. Rules are rules. Next time, be more careful to say that they *each* have to answer three questions. But don't worry—they won't be able to. They never can!"

The bridge troll appeared to cheer up at that. He must have been prepared for this, because he didn't hesitate. "How many straws go into a bird's nest?"

"What kind of bird?" Marabel asked.

The troll said, "It doesn't matter."

If it doesn't matter, Marabel thought, *then there isn't a real answer. It's a trick question, like a riddle.* She closed her eyes and thought.

Suddenly, Ellie said, "None."

"None?" the troll asked.

"None. Straws don't have feet. They can't go anywhere. So the answer to how many straws go into a bird's nest—or anywhere else—is none."

The three trolls behind her grunted in what sounded like disagreement, but the bridge troll was fair. "All right," he agreed. "That wasn't the answer I was looking for, but it makes sense, so I'll allow it. Hmm. Now, how about this one: How many calves' tails would you need to make a rope long enough to reach the moon?"

"Easy," Floriano said. The girls and the troll looked at

him. The unicorn swished his elegant tail. "Just one, if it's long enough."

"That's two!" Marabel squeezed Ellie's shoulder in delight. "Only one more to go!"

The bridge troll frowned at them and the other three growled low. "You'd better ask a good one," the biggest, ugliest troll warned. "If you let your first travelers cross without paying, you'll never get promoted." The trolls took a few steps closer and Marabel nearly gagged at their musty smell.

The bridge troll looked down at his feet, and then up at the sky. He tapped his lips with his finger as he thought.

"We don't have all day," Marabel said to him, and he waved a hand at her to hush.

Finally, he brightened. "I've got it!" He turned to the other trolls. "You're going to love this one!"

Marabel didn't like the sound of that.

The troll turned back to them, grinning. "What's my name?"

Stunned, Marabel took a step back. His *name*? How could she possibly know his name?

"That's not fair!" Ellie burst out, but Marabel knew there was no point in objecting. The rules didn't say anything about what kind of question he could ask.

The rules. The stupid, stupid, *stupid* rules. All her life

she'd lived by rules, by the Book, by the customs of Magikos. What good were rules anyway?

The three trolls moved forward menacingly. The big one licked his lips.

And then it hit her. She couldn't believe she hadn't thought of it before.

She looked straight at the bridge troll and grinned in triumph. "Your name is Paul," she said.

The three supervisor trolls burst out laughing. The bridge troll flushed green, and snapped, "That's not even close! Trolls don't have names like 'Paul'! We have names like Rumbleguts and Goateater."

"Too bad," Marabel said as regally as she could. "You said we had to answer three questions. We did, so let us cross."

"B-b-but—" the bridge troll stammered.

"You never said we had to answer them *correctly*. You just said answer them. Rules are rules, like you said. Come on, Ellie. Let's go, Floriano."

Ellie gave a little whimper as they passed the bridge troll. But Marabel strode by with her head held high and refused even to look at him. He looked stunned as he watched them go by. Floriano lifted his legs in a little prance and flicked his tail jauntily.

They were no more than halfway across when a great

yell made them jump. Ellie glanced back at the trolls and grabbed Marabel's arm.

"They're coming after us!" she shrieked, but before Marabel could answer, the bridge troll said to his supervisors, "You can't pass unless you *each* answer three questions, and answer them *correctly*," and the thud of big bony trollish feet on the wooden planks was replaced by indignant howls as the trolls argued.

Soon they were safely on the other side, and the sounds of the conflict faded, along with the roar of the rushing water. At last, they were on their way to Mab's castle.

And to Marco.

8

arabel, Ellie, and Floriano walked all day, so elated at their success with the bridge troll that they scarcely noticed how tired and hungry they were until the sun dropped low and their shadows lengthened. They found a sheltered spot near a stream, where the girls piled up pine needles and covered them with dry leaves to make beds. Floriano tiptoed to a spot near the two girls. Marabel smiled as he curled up and laid down his head.

From her pine-needle bed, Marabel watched the

stars coming out, and thought of the birthday banquet back home in the palace three days earlier.

Where are you, Marco? she wondered to herself. *Are you being fattened in a cage so Mab can eat you?* The idea of her gentle brother being tormented by their aunt was horrible. *I'm coming*, she thought. *I'll find you and rescue you—somehow—and we'll go home together.*

She turned over, restless. Had her father's messenger left for Mab's castle yet? What answer would Mab give him? Were both sides preparing for war even now? She couldn't imagine what that would be like. There hadn't been a war in Magikos for centuries, not since the time of King Malcolm and his great wizard, Callum.

A burst of distant laughter came to her.

I must be imagining things, Marabel thought. Who would be laughing in the middle of the night, in the middle of the forest? She turned over, pine needles pricking her, and closed her eyes, but it was hard to sleep when she was so hungry. It had been a long time since she'd eaten more than a few bites of bread and cheese.

Then she heard it again. Only this time, a strain of music accompanied the laughter. It sounded like a violin.

Marabel propped herself up on her elbows. *I'll go take a quick look*, she thought as she got up. *If it's something dangerous, I'll come back and wake up Floriano and Ellie so we can sneak away. No point in worrying them if it's nothing.*

She moved as silently as she could and hid behind a bush. Before her was a marvelous sight. In a clearing, musicians played drums, fiddles, and horns, the instruments beautifully reflecting firelight. People danced in a circle around the fire, laughing and talking, helping children make the correct steps, tripping over their own feet and laughing some more.

Marabel felt a hand touch her shoulder. Startled, she gasped and froze in place. The hand felt too heavy to be her friend's, but she whispered hopefully, "Ellie?" A soft chuckle, much deeper than any sound Ellie could make, was the response. Marabel looked down at her shoulder.

It was not a human hand. It was huge, and its fingers were long and bony, with sharp yellow claws instead of nails.

Marabel screamed.

The music stopped abruptly, and a babble broke out among the dancers: "What on earth was that?"

"Could you tell where it came from?"

"You don't think it's one of those banshees playing tricks again, do you?"

Marabel jerked free of the bony hand and tried to run away, but her feet refused to move. She stared up at the creature, unable to speak. She could barely see in the darkness, but it looked more or less like a person who had kept growing until it was far taller than any human, with pale orange skin that reflected the light of the moon. It was grimacing—no, it was grinning. It had long, knobby limbs, and its big head was topped by a mop of straw-like hair.

She wished she had paid more attention to her natural history lessons that covered the different sorts of Evils that roamed the Barrens. What *was* this? A goblin? An ogre? Something she'd never heard of?

"Nay, fair maiden, fear not," the strange-looking creature said. "'Twas but a jest. I humbly apologize for having affrighted you." And it made a surprisingly courtly bow.

"Ack," was all Marabel could say.

Then came the pounding of hooves and an indignant whinny as Floriano burst into the little clearing. He drew to a halt and said, "Hey! Leave her alone!"

The creature raised both hands in the air. "I intend no harm, Sir Unicorn," it said. "The lady mistook my intentions."

The bushes parted and a crowd peered at them. The curiosity on their faces quickly turned to amusement. A chubby little woman came bustling out of their midst. "Cornelius!" she scolded. "Have you been frightening people again?"

Soon Marabel was being served a very late supper while Floriano and Cornelius fetched Ellie.

"Please excuse Cornelius," the chubby little woman told Marabel as she set down a steaming bowl and a wooden spoon on the table in front of her. "He was merely playing a little joke and didn't think you'd be so frightened. He didn't know you were from the other side."

"The other side of what?" Marabel asked.

"You're from Magikos, aren't you? The kingdom that lies on the other side of the Wall, ruled by the evil King Matthew?"

Marabel thought she should defend her father, but she was afraid that she'd give herself away and jeopardize her quest, so instead she changed the subject. "You don't see many Magikians here?" She blew on a spoonful of stew. It smelled delicious.

"In my whole life I've only seen three," the woman answered. "One was a peddler who used to visit every spring when I was a girl. And to think that the second and third would come years later, and only a day apart!" She chuckled.

"I'm the third?" Marabel asked.

"You are."

"So the second was . . . ?"

"Someone from the other side, who came through the village only yesterday."

"Was it a human?" Marabel asked, her heart pounding.

"Oh yes. A man. Dressed all in blue and gold."

Marabel laid down her spoon. Her appetite had fled at the mention of the Magikian royal colors. It had to be her father's messenger. Marabel had known that the messenger would show up before too long, but it sounded like he had already gotten ahead of them. They had to hurry.

"What did he want?" she asked.

"He just asked the way to the castle. We were hoping it was something about our problem, but alas, no."

"What problem?" Marabel asked cautiously, hoping she wasn't being nosy.

Luckily, the woman seemed talkative. She sighed and sat down. "For several years now, we've been noticing that magical beings aren't behaving the way they used to. Why, when I was a girl you could walk through the woods without worrying about being trapped by a witch or snatched up by a dragon. Everyone mostly got along, magical or not. But those days are long gone. Magical beasts are acting strangely, and we don't know why. We were hoping that he was coming with some word about that, but as it turns out, he was only passing through."

Marabel picked up her spoon again. "Was he on horseback?"

"No, on foot, and Cornelius—my son, the one you met in the forest—said that he was complaining about blisters from his fancy shoes."

"Cornelius is your son?" Marabel was astonished. "Are you . . . I mean, you don't look . . ." She stopped.

"Oh, he's adopted," the lady said. "My husband and I—we're human beings, like you. But Cornelius was orphaned a few years ago, so we took him in."

"But isn't he . . . an ogre?"

"Of course! But that makes no difference to us. We love him." The woman ladled more stew into Marabel's bowl. "A child's a child. And he's a very good son."

"Cornelius is just a child?"

The woman chuckled. "He'd hardly appreciate being called that, but to me he is. I suppose he's a little older than you. What are you—twelve?"

"Thirteen." It was the first time Marabel had said that, and it made her think of the birthday banquet, and of Marco, with a pang. Her aunt might lose her temper and have Veneficus change Marco into a frog even before the thrennight was up. But there might be hope for them yet. If the messenger was on foot and if he already had blisters, they still had a chance of beating him to the castle, if they hurried. Slowly Marabel's appetite came back. And the stew was delicious—rich and savory with herbs.

She took a bite of brown bread and watched the dancing start up again. A silver unicorn joined the circle. Marabel marveled at how smoothly they all danced, humans and beasts together. A lady twined her fingers in the unicorn's mane, and the man on the unicorn's other side held on to an embroidered cloth that hung down from her horn. Nobody seemed surprised at the presence of the magical creature, and now that Marabel looked more carefully, she realized that the circle included at least one gnome and a few other non-humans.

Cornelius and Floriano returned, bringing with them a nervous-looking Ellie. Ellie's face relaxed when she saw Marabel dining happily, and she joined her at the table. So did Cornelius, who gulped down an entire roast chicken, bones and all, in two swallows. Floriano nibbled on an oat cake.

"Now that you've eaten," Cornelius's mother said, "why don't you tell me what you're doing here?"

Marabel was about to tell her everything when Ellie

gave a warning cough. Marabel hesitated, suddenly unsure she could trust this woman. She seemed nice enough, but what if she was in league with Mab? Even if she wasn't, she might betray them in hopes of a reward. So all she said was, "We've come on an adventure. We found a door in the woods, and Floriano opened it. We wanted to see what was on the other side." Not the whole truth, certainly, but none of it was a lie.

"You're Floriano?" the ogre's mother asked the unicorn. He nodded proudly, his mouth full of another oat cake, crumbs on his whiskers. "Ah, the horn of the unicorn is powerful," the woman said. "If only it were so easy to open the door from this side!"

"I would fain see the land of Magikos," Cornelius said wistfully. "It sounds like a wondrous place."

"A unicorn's horn isn't powerful enough to get you through to the Magikos side of the Wall?" Floriano asked. He looked insulted at this slur on the power of his horn.

"Not to go west to Magikos," the woman said. "The wicked Callum, who built the Wall, cast spells on it so that travelers coming east could pass through with little trouble, as long as they had one of your kind"—she nodded at Floriano—"or some undoing spell to unlock it. Magikians occasionally take advantage of that ease to come here to our side and kidnap our folk to gawk at them in cages." Marabel dropped her eyes, thinking of the delight that she and Marco had taken in their trips to the Wildlife Park. Had they been staring at caged creatures who should have been running free?

It was also strange to hear the great wizard Callum being called "wicked," especially right after Cornelius's mother had said her father was evil. Maybe from their point of view, Callum *was* wicked, and King Matthew *was* evil. It had never before occurred to Marabel that there might be another way to look at these things.

The woman concluded, "But for one of us to go to *your* side would take some very strong magic."

"Veneficus!" Marabel said.

The woman looked at her sharply. "Why do you mention the queen's wizard?" Oops—how could Marabel explain without giving away who she was?

Ellie rescued her. "If anyone could come up with strong magic, it would have to be a wizard like Veneficus, wouldn't it? That's all she meant."

Marabel put down her spoon, feeling wretched. If a unicorn's horn wasn't enough to open the door on the way back, how could they get home after they rescued Marco? Would they be forced to stay here forever? Maybe she should have done what her father had said and stayed home while he and his army took care of the problem. Was her quest hopeless?

Cornelius broke in, "Enough of this, fair companions! Let us join the merry throng of revelers." He stood and beckoned them to follow him to the circle of dancers.

Floriano said in Marabel's ear, "He talks like that all. The. *Time*. Thought I'd go crazy while we were fetching Ellie."

Marabel didn't feel like dancing, but she went to where a new circle was forming. A friendly dwarf took her right hand and tall Cornelius held her left. She soon caught on to the steps and twirled and stamped with the rest of them. Across the circle, Ellie hopped and pranced, her long golden braids bouncing, her face gleaming with sweat that reflected the firelight.

They danced for what felt like hours. Nobody told Marabel that what she was doing was undignified for a member of the royal family, no one told her to set a good example for the younger prince and princesses, and no one quoted the Book of Fate at her to make her stop doing something fun.

The music and the dancing and the friendliness of all the creatures made her spirits rise. *If it weren't for Marco being gone*, she thought as she collapsed, panting, onto the cool grass, *this would be the best night of my life.*

In a few minutes, Cornelius sat down next to her, his arms around his bony knees. "Verily, I am weary of the dance," he said, "and would beg to speak to you of your land. So few of our folk have ventured there that I am eager to know if the tales they tell are true."

"What have you heard?" Marabel asked, hoping he wouldn't want to know too much about Magikian geography or any of the other subjects that she hadn't paid much attention to.

"Do you really have a book whose commands you follow?" he asked. "Wonder of wonders! I long to see such a book."

"It doesn't really command us," Marabel said. "It just tells us what's going to happen."

Cornelius looked thoughtful. "In truth," he said, "I don't see much difference."

Come to think of it, Marabel didn't see much difference, either. She'd have to ask Symposia about it once they got home.

"Some have whispered that magic is forbidden in Magikos," Cornelius went on, "and that folk such as I would be imprisoned if we were found there. Do these people speak the truth?"

Marabel squirmed. She decided to be honest. "I don't know," she admitted. "I've never seen ... er, folk such as you in Magikos, so I don't know what would happen to you there.

And magic isn't forbidden, exactly. It's only that there are rules about how much you can use, and who can use it, and where."

"Indeed, there are such rules here, as well. Perhaps they are not as strict as yours, as the rules do get changed sometimes, if perchance a new method of spell casting is invented or some ancient art is revived and none are sure how it works."

Marabel was confused. "How do you change rules? Aren't rules always the same?"

It was Cornelius's turn to look baffled. "Nay, my lady, the people have the power and the will to modify them when necessary. Is it not so among the Magikians?"

Marabel didn't know how to explain. The Book and its teachings were so much a part of her life that she'd never had to think about them. "The Book of Fate—it's a book, well, obviously it's a book—and it tells us everything important that's going to happen," she stumbled. "It knows everything."

"A mere book knows everything?" Cornelius said. "It must be a magical book!"

"Oh no," Marabel said. "It's not magic, but it's very wise. It's written in an ancient language that's hard to understand, and I think that sometimes it's possible the priests get things wrong." She hoped so anyway. If the priests were right about Marco rescuing himself, then Marabel's quest was a dangerous waste of time.

"I intend no disrespect to this ancient and learnèd tome," Cornelius said, "but perhaps the priests read only what they wish to see in it?"

It had never occurred to Marabel that the priests might twist the Book's words to suit their own ends. The thought was so new and strange that she didn't know how to answer.

When the music and the dancing died down, Cornelius showed Marabel to a hut that held several small beds and was well stocked with food and water. It was the custom in this area, he said, to welcome visitors, and to give them a comfortable place to stay. She spotted Ellie, curled up on one of the beds.

"The maiden who accompanied you is already deep in slumber, as you can see. Your unicorn friend is in yon field with some of his brethren." Cornelius pointed to where Marabel could just make out large one-horned shapes scattered across the dark meadow. "If you require naught else, I will bid you good night."

Marabel tucked her wooden sword under her pillow for safekeeping and lay down on the bed next to Ellie's. It was so warm and soft that she didn't even have time to worry about the king's messenger before she, too, fell into a deep sleep.

9

The next morning, Cornelius's mother tried to get them to stay and rest a few days, but Marabel politely refused. The thought of that messenger, already a day ahead of them, made her anxious, and she didn't even wait for full light before they thanked their hosts and headed back into the woods.

Four long, weary days of trudging through the forest passed, and once again they were hungry. Cornelius's mother had made sure that they were well laden with food when they left the village, but walking all day made them ravenous and they had gone through almost all of it in three days.

At first, this didn't worry them. They cut way back on what they ate at every meal, and were sure they'd happen on more food soon. But it seemed that this part of the Barrens lived up to its name; the fields were almost bare, and they saw no magical creatures and very few people. All they had left to eat were a few small apples they had happened upon in an abandoned orchard. Floriano, of course, had plenty to graze on, and the many streams and ponds of the Barrens kept them from being thirsty, but Marabel was getting anxious. And hungry.

"Isn't there any more?" Marabel asked after they had eaten an apple each, and a few bites of bread and cheese, on the eighth morning after leaving the palace.

"Half an apple left. Enough for one mouthful each for lunch." Ellie carefully wrapped a clean leaf around the small piece of fruit and tucked it into her hood, which hung down her back. She stood and gently nudged Marabel with her toe. "Come on."

"One more minute," Marabel said. Her legs and back ached.

"'The cat that sleeps all day catches no mice,'" Ellie quoted from the Book of Fate.

Marabel pushed herself up and rose to her feet. "What does the Book know about walking all day without eating more than a shriveled apple? And who wants to catch mice anyway?" she grumbled.

They trudged through the forest until the sun was high in the sky. Marabel couldn't go on. "Enough," she said. "Time to take a break." All she could think about was that mouthful of apple.

Floriano immediately put down his head and cropped at the grass, and Marabel looked expectantly at Ellie. But when Ellie reached into her hood, she found nothing there. "What happened to it?" she asked frantically, digging her hand in deeper.

Marabel reached her own hand all the way into Ellie's hood. "Ellie!" She thought she was going to cry with hunger and frustration. "What did you do? How could you lose our only . . ." She bit her lip. Harsh words wouldn't bring the apple back.

"Let's look on the trail," Ellie said. "Maybe the apple fell out on that last scramble up the hill."

They searched everywhere. They poked through piles of leaves and under shrubs. No apple. Finally, they had to give up.

"I'm sorry," Ellie said, looking guilty. "I don't know what

happened. It must have fallen out of my hood when we were climbing over that big rock, or maybe when I slipped in the mud next to the stream." Both of those places were too far to go back to, especially on an empty stomach.

"It doesn't matter," Marabel said wearily, but her words were interrupted by a long growl from her belly. She tried not to care—Marco, after all, was probably being fed moldy bread and dirty moat water in some dungeon—but the thought of walking for who knew how much farther without anything to eat was daunting.

Ellie looked even guiltier than before and said, "Let's go on. Maybe we'll find some nuts or something."

They fought their way through the underbrush until, by sheer luck, they came upon another path. They were a little cheered by how much easier it was to walk there and especially by the thought that a path meant they might be approaching a town. They hurried on, only to come out of the woods . . . not in a town, but on the edge of a cliff. The path continued on to a thin, swaying rope bridge that hung over a wide chasm. This deep crack curved in a wide arc around a mountain, but the misty air made it hard to see the other side.

"What do we do now?" Floriano asked.

"I say we go back and see if we missed a fork in the path,"

Ellie said. "That bridge doesn't look strong enough to hold all of us. Surely this can't be the only way."

Marabel hesitated. She wasn't particularly afraid of heights, but the chasm was so deep and the bridge looked so spindly. No trolls were in sight this time, though, which was something.

"We have to go on if we want to get to the castle ahead of the messenger," she said.

Floriano grumbled, but he followed as Marabel and then Ellie stepped onto the bridge. After one sickening glance over the side, Marabel kept her eyes straight ahead. A few fat birds swooped close overhead. They hovered, making a strange buzzing sound like giant hummingbirds, and then flew on. Distant rumblings of thunder made them quicken their steps, but the sky remained a clear blue, and no lightning flashed.

As they got closer, they saw that the deep crack entirely circled the mountain. When they finally stepped off the bridge onto the ground, their legs were trembling.

But the path didn't reappear on this side. The forest looked different here, somehow. The tree trunks were green and smooth, and other tall, thin plants towered over them.

Ellie was staring up one of the trees. "What on earth?" she muttered. Marabel craned her neck back and followed her gaze. An enormous flower was at the top of the tree. It looked like a daisy, only it was as big as a bed.

Floriano had raised his head, too, his flared nostrils sniffing the air. Marabel looked at him questioningly.

He sniffed again. "I smell food, I think." One long ear twitched. "But I don't hear anything. I don't think anyone's here."

Food? Marabel forgot all about the strange flower tree. "I'm going to go look," she said. "You two wait here."

"Oh, no you don't!" Ellie grabbed Marabel's sleeve. "It's not normal for there to be food in the middle of the forest, especially with nobody around. Have you forgotten where we are? The Desolate Barrens! It's full of Evils. Why, they could have laid a trap! They might be waiting for somebody to come by and eat their porridge or—"

"Don't be silly," Marabel said. "All I'm going to do is look. You can stay here where it's safe, if you don't want to come with me."

"Sounds good to me," Floriano put in. "Go check it out and report back. If you meet someone friendly, ask them if they have any oats. A steady diet of grass is going to give me indigestion."

"No," Ellie said firmly. "Not going to happen. We're not splitting up. Either we're all going or none of us are going."

"I vote none," Floriano said.

"Fine," Marabel said. "Do what you want. I'm going."

She strode off without looking back. After a few minutes, she heard hurried footsteps behind her, and Ellie slipped her hand into Marabel's.

"My mother told me—"

"Always to stay with me," Marabel finished for her. "But if you're really scared, Ellie, you don't have to."

"I'm no more scared than you are," Ellie retorted.

Having Ellie by her side gave Marabel new confidence. Together, the two of them crept toward the source of the delicious smell. They entered a clearing and what they saw left them speechless: An enormous, red-and-white-checkered blanket was spread out on the ground, covered with plates and bowls heaped with steaming mounds of food. Slices of crusty bread towered in piles higher than their heads. There was a platter of what looked like roasted vegetables, frosty pitchers full of pink liquid, and other things that they couldn't identify.

"Do you hear that?" Ellie hissed.

Marabel held still. Sure enough, she heard a low, rumbling sound. Suddenly, Marabel realized what she was looking at. Her heart began to pound. What she had thought was a hill was actually a huge bearded man, lying on his back. As she watched, wide-eyed, his chest rose and let out another rumble.

It was a giant, and he was snoring.

Ellie tugged at the sleeve of Marabel's garb. "Let's go!" she whispered. "What if he wakes up? The Book says, 'Never wake a sleeping giant.'"

But Marabel couldn't take her eyes off all that food. "You stay here," she told Ellie. "I'm going to get us something to eat." She moved Ellie's clinging hand off her shoulder, patted it, and tiptoed into the clearing. At each step, she thought about tales of giants eating humans. Could that be true? Could the plates be full of . . . roasted people? Just as Marabel was about to turn back, Ellie shrieked. It looked like she was caught in the branch of a tree . . . a tree wearing a pair of overalls. Marabel realized that the tree was a child—a huge child—clutching a squirming Ellie in one of her fists.

"Papa!" the young giant girl bellowed as she thudded past Marabel. "Papa! Look what I found!"

Her father sat up, his immense head blocking the sun. "Fee fi fo fum," he said through a yawn, stretching his arms out so wide that Marabel winced at their size. "What have you found, darling?"

The giant girl held Ellie out. Her father cupped his hands and the girl dropped her.

This time, Marabel couldn't hold back a scream as Ellie plummeted into the giant's hand. Instantly, something seized her around the waist. She'd been grabbed by another giant girl. Marabel fought and wiggled, trying to pry open the fingers squeezing her so hard that she could barely breathe. Her captor laughed with delight and ran to the other giants, making Marabel's head bounce.

"Papa! I have one, too!"

"Why, so you do," he boomed. "One each! How lovely! Here, put them in this." He opened the top of an enormous picnic basket and dropped Ellie and Marabel into it. He inspected them, wafting billows of horrible-smelling giant breath into the basket, before closing the top. Marabel and Ellie clung together in the sudden darkness.

"This is some kind of giant land," Ellie said, her voice trembling. "Those big 'trees' we saw when we got off the bridge? They were giant flowers, not trees at all."

"And the other plants must have been giant blades of grass," Marabel said. "And those birds that buzzed over us on the bridge—giant bees." She shuddered at the thought of what would have happened if one of them had been stung.

"My dear!" the giant called, and even though his voice was muffled by the basket, the girls winced at the sound. "Come see what the children have found, the little darlings!"

123

BOOM, BOOM, BOOM. Marabel realized that what they'd been hearing earlier hadn't been thunder, but gigantic footsteps.

The top of the basket opened and four gigantic heads peered down at them. "How *sweet!*" the mother giant cooed. She reached in an enormous hand and stroked first Marabel's head and then Ellie's with a heavy finger.

Marabel mustered all her courage. "Are . . . are you going to eat us?" she quavered.

One of the girls said, "Ew!" and the other made a theatrical gagging sound.

The giant mother drew back with an expression of horror. "*Eat* you? What a thought! No, never! We're vegans, all of us. We've never let a morsel of meat cross our lips." The other three heads nodded vigorously in agreement. "Why don't you share our lunch with us?" the woman suggested. "We have so few visitors, and due to the canyon that goes around our mountain home, we rarely get the chance to meet people. Do join us!"

"Share your lunch with you?" Marabel asked uncertainly. If giants didn't eat people, what *did* they eat?

The giant father said, "We have a lovely kale and quinoa salad, some homemade bread, lemonade—"

"Hummus!" one of the girls exclaimed.

"Roasted veggies!" said the other one.

Marabel and Ellie exchanged glances. It sounded good after three days of eating only what they could carry and then two days of just about no food. "Thank you," Marabel said uncertainly.

The giant father lifted them out of the basket and set them on the blanket, the giant girls perched uncomfortably close. Ellie flinched as an enormous foot barely missed her when one of the girls crossed her legs. "Abigail and Sophia," their mother said, "be careful. Don't hurt them, and do your best not to make them nervous, the little dears."

"Where's—" Marabel began, looking around and wondering where Floriano had gotten to. But Ellie jabbed her in the ribs with her elbow, and she stopped short.

"Where's what?" asked one of the girls—Abigail or Sophia.

"Where's the, um, salt?" Marabel squeaked.

"Salt is poison," the mother giant said as she scooped up what must have been, to her, a tiny portion of salad. "We never add salt." She rummaged around, evidently looking for something small enough for Marabel and Ellie to use as a plate, but gave up and carefully placed the spoon on the blanket.

The kale and quinoa salad was delicious, although the

dressing made it messy to eat with their fingers. Along with salt, the giants evidently didn't believe in sugar, either, and the lemonade, while flavored with berries that made it a pretty pink, puckered their mouths so much that Marabel and Ellie couldn't drink more than a sip. The bread, though, was chewy and crusty. Enough hummus to fill a bathtub overflowed from a bowl.

When they had eaten all they could, Marabel and Ellie rose to their feet. They performed their best curtseys, and Abigail and Sophia squealed, "They're so *cute!*"

Marabel said, "Thank you for the delicious lunch. But now we have to go."

All four giant faces turned to them in surprise.

"Go?" said Papa Giant.

"Go?" said the two girl giants.

"Go?" said Mama Giant. "You're not going anywhere!"

10

"What do you mean, we're not going anywhere?" Marabel was bewildered. "We *have* to go." Blistered or not, her father's messenger was probably well on his way to Mab's castle by now.

But the father giant shook his head. "Much too dangerous out there for such little things," he said. "Besides, haven't you seen how fond of you our children already are?" The girls beamed at Marabel and Ellie.

"We like your children very much, too," Marabel said uncertainly. "And we thank you for the lovely lunch, and for telling us about salt. But we must take our leave now."

She might as well not have said anything. The giants didn't answer, except to laugh the way people do when a dog or a monkey does something that looks human.

The giant mother scooped up Marabel and Ellie, accidentally knocking their heads together, and put them in her satchel. She slung it over her shoulder, flinging them around, and then with a cheery "Time to go, girls!" she started walking.

"What do we do now?" wailed Ellie, rubbing her head. Her knee was in Marabel's face. Marabel pushed it away and tried to haul herself up over a pile of tissues, a huge lipstick, a mirror that made her look like something from a nightmare, and enormous coins that clanked together, threatening to bruise them both. The bag swayed and bumped with the giant's steps, and Marabel had barely poked her head out when the movement caught the giant woman's attention. The giant zipped her satchel shut. "Little scamp!" her voice boomed far overhead, followed by a chuckle.

Every step their captor took jolted Marabel and Ellie, and the enclosed space soon became warm and stuffy. It smelled like some kind of fake leather.

"Let me out!" Ellie's voice was panicky. She moaned and added, "I think I'm going to be sick."

"Oh no!" Marabel was torn between worry over Marco, fear that Ellie was going to throw up, and concern for Floriano. Luckily, just as Ellie clamped her hands over her mouth, the giant woman put her purse down with a thud, unzipped the top, and lifted the girls out, tangling their limbs together again. She dropped them on a broad wooden expanse, which Marabel realized was a tabletop. She jumped to her feet and looked around at the cavernous room as Ellie lay still, her clammy face slowly regaining its color.

The picnic basket was stowed in a nearby corner, and the rest of the room was filled with huge toys, books, and paper. It looked a lot like Marabel and Marco's old playroom.

The relatively fresh air and the lack of motion seemed to revive Ellie, who sat up and pushed her damp hair out of her face, breathing shallowly.

"Now let's find them a nice box to live in," the giant mother said. "You have to be gentle, girls, and be careful not to break them the way you did your last pets."

Break them? Last pets? Marabel and Ellie looked at each other with dread.

"I want the yellow-headed one!" said the taller of the two girls.

"Mama!" wailed the other one. "Sophia wants mine! *I* was the one who found the yellow-headed one! She found the other one!"

"Hush, darlings," their mother said. "You can share them." That set off another round of wailing, which the woman ignored. She picked up Marabel and Ellie, even though they kicked and squirmed, and put them in a box with high sides. She ripped up some paper and covered the bottom with it, and then carefully placed what looked like a doll's china bowl, which was as large as a real one to Marabel and Ellie, in one corner. She filled it with water and stepped back.

"Now, leave them alone for a little while," the mother said. "They might cry the first few nights, like the others, but they'll soon quiet down. I'm sure you'll have lots of fun with them as long as they last. Don't take them out of their box, mind! Remember what happened with the gnome you found?"

"He ran away," the shorter one—Abigail—said mournfully.

"We never found him," Sophia added with a quaver.

"That's right." Their mother nodded. "This box will have to do for tonight, and tomorrow I'll find a better one. And mind, you're going to have to feed them and exercise them and clean up after their messes. I'm not going to do it for you."

She hurried from the room, ignoring Marabel's frantic calls of "Wait!"

Ellie, wild-eyed, grabbed Marabel's arm. "What did she mean, 'a better box'? Do you think she meant one with doors and windows, that we could get out of when we wanted?"

"Probably," Marabel said to calm Ellie's fears. "Although I bet she means something sturdier, too."

She was more worried about something else the giant mother had said: "as long as they last." She shivered and kicked at the wall, and it wobbled. "What's this made of, anyway—some kind of paper?"

"Who cares what it's made of?" Ellie said forlornly. "Whatever it is, it's much too hard for us to break it."

The giant girls had fallen silent and were staring at them eagerly. "What do *you* want?" Marabel asked, not caring how rude she sounded.

What the girls wanted, it turned out, was to play with them. Abigail picked up Marabel, and Sophia picked up Ellie, and the giant girls "walked" them across the table and onto the floor, gripping them around their middles and bouncing them along. Sophia said in a squeaky voice, "Thank you for coming to my tea party!" and Abigail said,

"Thank you for inviting me!" Marabel and Ellie struggled to stand, but it was difficult in the knee-deep, itchy rug.

The giant girls set up a crude wooden table and four chairs. They put a stuffed mouse on one rickety chair and a toy troll on another. They set the table with lumpy teacups, and saucers and plates full of toy food that looked disgusting.

They played tea party, and then they played dress-up. They were in the middle of a game when Abigail let out a gaping yawn, showing monstrous teeth and a tongue the size of a bedspread, and rubbed her eyes. She dropped Ellie onto the rug—luckily from a height of only a few feet—and said, "This is getting boring."

Sophia said, "What do you want to do now?" She, too, yawned. Her eyelids looked heavy.

The yawning gave Marabel an idea. She didn't know whether it would work (or if it did work, whether it would help them), but it was the only thing she could think of.

"Do you want me to tell you a story?" she asked as brightly as she could manage.

"A story?" Sophia asked doubtfully. Ellie, too, looked skeptical.

"Oh yes," Marabel said. "It's a famous story in . . . in the place we come from. I don't know if you're old enough to understand it, though."

The giant girls looked indignant. "We are, too, old enough!" Abigail said, as Marabel had hoped she would. "We're older than you!"

From the way they'd been behaving, Marabel had her doubts, but she merely sighed. "Well, I can try, but you'll have to keep your eyes closed so you can picture everything in your mind."

The girls looked at each other and shrugged. "All right," Sophia said. She dropped Marabel and Ellie back in the box, sloshing water out of the little bowl and bruising both of them.

Oh no, Marabel thought. *This ruins everything.* Out loud she said, "Can you take us out again, please?"

"You have to stay in your box," Sophia retorted. "Mama said."

Marabel refrained from pointing out that they had been out of the box all afternoon playing giant games, despite instructions from "Mama."

"All right," she said. "This is fine. Now close your eyes so you can concentrate."

They did. Abigail disappeared from view, and Marabel, who couldn't see over the high edge of the box, fervently hoped that she had laid her head on her arms. This tale from the Book of Fate was supposed to be about persistence, but she didn't know how it ended. She'd always fallen asleep before the teller got that far.

"Once upon a time, a little crab lived at the bottom of the ocean. Now, this little crab was always afraid of being eaten by something larger, and almost everything in the ocean was larger than the little crab.

"So one day, the little crab decided to build himself a sturdy house. He found a nice spot and put pebbles in a circle as the current moved back and forth, back and forth, so slowly. . . ." Sophia's eyelids drooped, but as soon as Marabel paused, they sprang open again. "Seeing no more pebbles, the little crab tiptoed out onto the sand on his sharp claws. He picked up two more pebbles and walked back to his shelter, and dropped the pebbles into the circle. He walked back out a little farther and found two more pebbles." Sophia's eyes closed again, and this time they didn't open. Marabel continued softly, "He walked back and dropped them."

A snore made her pause. One of the giant girls was asleep. But were both of them? She looked over at Ellie, who called quietly, "Abigail!" No answer. "Sophia!" Still nothing. "They must be asleep," she whispered. "But how are we going to get out?"

"Maybe we can break the walls after all," Marabel said

quietly. "The mother did say something about a gnome getting away."

"Gnomes carry trowels and shovels and things." Ellie gave the wall an experimental push. "How can we poke through it without some kind of tool?"

"Oh!" Marabel picked up the bowl and tossed the water that remained at the wall. The wall soaked up the water and turned dark, and when Marabel pressed it, it felt soggy. But it appeared that giant paper was much thicker than human paper, and her fist still couldn't go through.

Maybe if both of them threw their weight against one wall, they could tip the box over? She didn't think they'd succeed, and it would make a lot of noise, which might wake up Sophia and Abigail. Or—

"Marabel?" Ellie said.

"Wait a second, Ellie! I'm thinking."

"But, Marabel, your *sword*!" Ellie pointed at the wet wall.

Marabel looked down at her waist. "Do you think it's sharp enough?" she asked doubtfully.

"We don't have anything else to try," replied the practical Ellie.

Marabel drew the sword. If she broke it, Lucius would be angry, but if she didn't try, he'd never see it again anyway. So she clutched its wooden grip and stabbed at the wall where the water had softened it.

Instantly, the blade went through the cardboard, almost up to its hilt. Marabel was surprised at how easily it penetrated. She yanked it out of the wall and made another hole, and then another, outlining an opening. She was afraid that Sophia and Abigail would wake up, but the giant girls' steady breathing continued.

"You're getting tired," Ellie said. "Let me help."

Marabel handed over the sword. But to Marabel's astonishment, when Ellie made a quick thrust at the wall, the sword bounced off it, leaving only a dent. "Maybe the water hasn't softened it there," Marabel suggested.

Ellie tried again, with no luck.

"That's so strange. It worked fine for me." Marabel took the sword and jabbed at the wall. It went through as cleanly as her other cuts. She finished and aimed a kick at the weakened paper. The piece popped out. Success!

Ellie crawled through the small opening. Marabel followed and flinched at Abigail's huge face right in front of her. The giant girl didn't move, but continued with her regular breathing, now accompanied by a whistle through her nose.

They lowered themselves onto a chair and then the floor, cringing at each little noise. Marabel's spirits lifted and her exhaustion fled. They'd find Floriano somehow, and run as fast as they could, and surely they'd be out of giant territory in no time. Then they'd find the castle and . . .

She bumped into Ellie, who had stopped short. "What?" Marabel asked in a whisper. She followed Ellie's gaze upward.

The door leading out of the playroom was shut, and the doorknob was far, far above their heads.

Ellie's shoulders slumped and Marabel felt like crying with frustration. Trying not to show her discouragement, she said firmly, "We'll have to build stairs or a ramp or something."

"Mara, look!" Ellie whispered. She pointed at a box that was illustrated with a picture of colorful building blocks like the ones Marabel and Marco had played with when they were little.

The girls opened the box and worked feverishly to build a staircase. They clambered up each step as soon as they had it in place, hauling more blocks up with them. In a short time, a flight of steps stood under the door handle. Marabel stood on tiptoe and stretched up.

Once again, she was smacked down with frustration. She could reach just fine now, but the knob was smooth and perfectly round. Ellie tried, too, but neither one could get a good enough grip to make it budge even a little.

"*Plague* it!" Marabel spat, not caring if she woke up Abigail and Sophia. At this point, it didn't matter.

From below came an amused voice. "Need some help?"

Marabel nearly lost her balance with surprise. She peered over the edge of their block staircase and saw a familiar head poking out of the picnic basket.

Floriano!

He climbed out of the basket and yawned, stretching his legs. "I snuck into the basket while you were having lunch with those giants. There was another whole box full of salad in there. What a feast! But then I fell asleep. I woke up a little while ago and heard the girls playing with you. It didn't sound like you were having much fun." He snorted a horse laugh.

Marabel and Ellie gestured frantically, pointing at the giant girls.

"What?" Floriano looked around, and gave a great start when he saw Abigail and Sophia. He leaped away from them and galloped to the foot of the staircase. "I could tell from their voices that they were big, but I didn't know they were *that* big!" he said more quietly, his star-shaped pupils enormous. "I thought they left while you were telling that crab story. *I* would have. It was the most boring thing I ever heard. What if they wake up? Why don't we get out of here?"

"That's what we're trying to do," Marabel hissed down at him. "But we can't open the door!"

"Gee, wouldn't it be great if you knew a lock-opening magical beast?" Floriano said, rolling his eyes. He surveyed the door, and once again his horn glowed. He reared up in the air and came down, dragging his horn along the crack between the door and the wall.

They waited for the latch to click open. Nothing. Floriano gave an impatient snort and tried again. He stamped his hoof when, once again, the door stayed firmly shut.

"Maybe you have to do it up here, where it latches," Ellie called down softly. "Come on up and try."

"All right," he said. He climbed the steps, the girls wincing at every tap of each golden hoof. When he reached them, he said, more seriously than they had ever heard him speak before, "You girls go back down and get ready to run out the door. Don't wait for me—I'll catch up."

"Be careful!" Marabel said as she and Ellie hurried down the steps.

But Floriano wasn't listening. His horn glowed, and he pawed the ground. The girls jumped off the last step onto the rug at the same instant that the unicorn reared high, high up. With the tip of his horn, he tapped the door right where it was latched.

With a loud *click*, the knob turned and the door popped open, knocking over the blocks and tossing Floriano into the air. He let out a surprised whinny, and landed on the thick rug with a thud. He didn't stir. Was he dead?

Marabel was about to run to him when Abigail raised her head and blinked, so she held herself back with difficulty. She tried desperately to see if the unicorn was breathing, but she couldn't tell. What was Abigail doing?

The giant girl peered into the cardboard box. They held their breath as she shook the box slightly, thankful the hole was on the opposite side from where she was looking. Evidently satisfied that the lumps of shredded paper were actually Marabel and Ellie, Abigail put her head back down on her arms.

Floriano raised his head and looked around, blinking. He appeared confused, but in a moment his eyes cleared. Marabel pressed her hand to her heart in relief.

Marabel and Ellie ran to him, their footfalls muffled by the rug, and helped him to his feet. "You did it, Floriano!" Marabel whispered, and then they hurried out the open door.

The girls had entered the house inside a satchel, and Floriano had been closed in the picnic basket, so they didn't know which way led out. Keeping close to the walls, they hurried down one long corridor after another without finding anything that looked like a door to the outer world, until finally they saw a giant woman dressed in a maid's uniform go by, carrying a bucket. Ellie nudged Marabel. "We have to follow her," she whispered. "She's going outside to dump the mop water."

Marabel hung back. Following someone down this empty corridor would be risky, with so few places to hide. "How do you know she isn't going someplace else to clean another floor?"

"It's the end of the day," Ellie said. "Trust me; I know how servants clean a house. She's done for the day."

They ran after the maid and caught up with her as she opened a side door, letting in late-afternoon light. They watched, all three huddled together in a shadow, as she swung the bucket in a big arc and tossed out its contents. A plume of water, higher than the largest waterfall in Magikos, flew into the air and splashed on the ground. The maid turned and went back inside. Before she closed the door, Marabel, Ellie, and Floriano sped through the opening and down the steps. They ran across the yard, faster than they had ever run in their lives.

Marabel thought she heard a distant bellow of "Mama!" followed by a shout of "Papa!"

"Faster!" she gasped. But how far away was the bridge? They hadn't been bounced around in the giant mother's bag for very long, but her enormous strides might have carried them miles away, even in that short time.

"This way!" Floriano cried. The girls followed him onto a rope bridge that bounced and swayed and bobbed as they sped across it.

The other side was tantalizingly close, when a sudden jolt tossed them in the air. The girls grabbed the ropes, but Floriano nearly went over the side. He whinnied in terror as Marabel clutched his horn and Ellie grasped his tail. Marabel looked back and saw a horrible sight: the giant father shaking the end of the bridge and yelling at them in rage.

Holding the unicorn steady between them, the girls each kept one hand on the railing and took off as fast as they could while the bridge swayed and bucked beneath their feet.

"I don't . . . think . . . I can . . . do this . . . much . . . longer," Floriano gasped.

"You have to!" Marabel called back over her shoulder. "We're almost there!"

Finally, they arrived at the other side. They leaped off onto the nice, solid cliff and didn't stop running until they were well within the shelter of the trees, sure at every moment that they were going to hear the *BOOM, BOOM, BOOM* of giant footsteps behind them. But all they heard were their own gasps and footfalls, and the squirrels and birds and the wind in the trees.

After they had all caught their breath, Ellie asked anxiously, "Do you think they'll come looking for us?"

"They can't fit on that bridge," Marabel said, "and even *they* aren't big enough to step across the canyon." She shuddered at the thought that enough people—and probably a lot of magical beasts as well—had crossed that bridge that they'd beaten out a path to the giants' mountain. How could Mab allow such danger in her land? She called herself the ruler of the Barrens, so she should make it a safe place for its citizens!

All Marabel wanted right now was to stay here, resting in the nice green forest with its normal-sized trees and normal-sized flowers and bugs and grass, but time was getting short. Only five days of the thrennight remained.

They had to move on. Marabel got to her feet and glanced at the sky.

"Huh." The others looked, too.

"What is it?" Ellie asked.

"We're on the other side of the mountain from where

we started," Marabel said. "That must have been a different bridge than the first one we crossed. See?" She pointed at the sun, now clearly visible through the leaves. "We're to the east of the mountain now. We crossed the first bridge from the west onto the giants' land, and then went to their house"—Ellie shuddered at the mention—"and then we crossed *this* bridge, and now we're on the other side."

"That puts us closer to the castle!" Ellie said.

Marabel nodded. "A lot closer. We might actually get there in time!" She grinned, and Ellie grinned back at her.

"Let's see if we can find a road going the right way, or at least another path, before night falls," Floriano suggested.

After they had walked for a few minutes, Floriano snorted. "Don't you wish you could have seen those girls' faces when they realized you were gone?"

Ellie broke into a laugh. It was the first time in what felt like ages that any of them had laughed. Marabel joined in, and Floriano whickered. "And that mother!" Ellie mimicked the giant woman. "'Go? You're not going anywhere!' We showed *her*!"

"'Don't break them like you broke the other ones!'" Marabel said. "Ha!" The relief of being safe and on the road again made her giddy.

Their bellies were full, they had escaped the giants, and several hours of daylight still remained. Surely their luck had changed, and they'd find a road that led to Mab's castle before nightfall.

Surely.

11

They carried on for four more days without seeing a road, much less a path or even another sign-post. Anxiety gnawed at Marabel's insides. She didn't know how far they were from her aunt's castle, and she had no idea how they would rescue Marco once they arrived.

A squirrel chittered at them. They thought it might be trying to tell them something, but when they tried to talk to it, it spiraled up a tree and vanished from sight.

They were tired and hungry and needed to stop frequently. It grew more and more difficult to convince

Floriano to get up after each break. "I don't see what's the big hurry," he complained when they practically had to hoist him to his feet after a rest late in the day. "We still have two days to get there, and we must be close by now. Why not stop and find a place to sleep?"

"We have to keep going," Marabel said. "Even if we get to the castle soon, we don't know how long it will take to find Marco and free him."

"Oh, Book give me patience," Floriano said. "You're not going to be able to free him!"

Marabel stopped short and turned to glare at him. "What do you mean? What are we doing out here, then?"

"Beats me," Floriano said. "I'm just along for the adventure. The rest is your problem, not mine. And speaking of problems, didn't you tell me that Mab has a powerful wizard working for her?"

"She does," Marabel said, although admitting it made her uneasy.

"I don't think you'll be able to waltz in, ask her, 'Please, Auntie, where's my brother?' and stroll out with him."

"We're going to do something." Marabel hoped she sounded more confident than she felt. "I can't leave him there." She strode off, followed by Ellie. She refused to look back to see if Floriano was coming. She didn't want to admit, even to herself, how anxious his words made her.

"Wait!" Floriano called after them.

Marabel and Ellie didn't answer. "I don't want to listen to him anymore," Marabel said, worry making her grumpy. "If he wants to take a rest, he can catch up later."

"Guys, I see something in the woods!" the unicorn called, more urgently this time.

"What is it?" Marabel called back reluctantly. She didn't stop; she was sure he was just making an excuse to take a break.

"Something pretty!" His voice faded as the girls continued on their way. "Come see!"

"*Sure* he found something pretty," Ellie scoffed.

"Something imaginary, more like," Marabel agreed. "Let's keep going."

"It'll be nice not to have to listen to him complaining," Ellie said.

But after they had continued on for another few hundred yards, Marabel began to feel guilty. Floriano had dropped behind before, but never for this long.

She stopped. "I guess we have to go back and look for him," she said reluctantly.

They called him, but nothing—not even an echo—

answered. Marabel tried to tell herself that if he was lost it wasn't her fault, but that didn't help. She knew she should have made sure they all stayed together.

"Where do you think he got to?" Ellie asked.

Before Marabel could answer, she heard the welcome sound of hooves on dry leaves, and a flash of pale blue and gold between the trees. Floriano trotted up to them. Marabel sighed in relief.

"Dear girls!" the unicorn said with a flash of his bright teeth, in what looked like a grin.

Marabel and Ellie exchanged glances. *Dear girls?* He had never called them anything like that before! What was he up to?

"Sorry to keep you waiting," he went on. "The day is so delightful that I quite lost track of time."

"Um . . . That's all right," Marabel said. He sounded so weirdly cheerful. Also, something about him looked different, but she couldn't figure out what it was. He was the same size as always, and the same colors, and his horn was in the same place, but still, something was off.

"And the truth is," he said, "that I found the most *charming* thing down the hill. Come along and I'll show you. You'll be spellbound." He switched his tail and turned back the way he had come. He looked at them over his shoulder, and it seemed that a flicker of annoyance crossed his face before it smoothed out into an unfamiliar blandness. "Why, what are you waiting for?"

"What is this . . . charming thing?" Ellie asked.

"Oh, I can't describe it," he said with a light laugh. "You'll have to see for yourselves! But you'll be quite enchanted; you'll see." And he set off again.

The girls glanced at each other. Marabel shrugged and said quietly, "What harm could it do to go back a little way?"

"I don't like it," Ellie said. "He's not behaving like himself."

"He's just acting strange because of our quarrel," Marabel said, to convince herself more than Ellie. "Let's go a little ways with him, and then we can come back."

"La-a-a-dies!" Floriano called in his new, oddly sweet voice. "I'm waiting!"

Marabel started toward him, but Ellie grabbed her arm. "No!" she said. "I'm serious, Marabel. There's something wrong. Did you hear what he said when he was describing this . . . this *thing*?"

"He didn't really describe it," Marabel said. "All he said was that it was charming."

"And that we'd be enchanted and spellbound," Ellie added. "Charms? Enchantment? Spells?"

Marabel couldn't believe what her friend was saying.

"Are you trying to tell me that he's seen something magical that will cast a spell over us? You don't really think that Floriano—"

Right on cue, the unicorn reappeared. His nostrils flared. "Is there some problem?" He looked from Marabel to Ellie and back again.

And then Marabel realized what was different. "His eyes!" she cried, tugging Ellie back. "His eyes! They're not stars—they're regular round pupils!"

As the words left her lips, Floriano disappeared in a sudden green flash and a puff of smoke. In his place there now stood a tall, elegant man with a dark, curled mustache and a pointy little beard. He was dressed in flowing robes of beautiful shades of blue and purple, and his hat was decorated with feathers that flashed in the sun.

"You—you little *brats*!" he shouted. "You destroyed my beautiful magic!"

"Who are you?" Marabel asked, striding toward him with clenched fists. "What have you done with Floriano?"

The man slid backward into the woods. He grabbed at branches and shrubs, but they slipped from his grasp as he continued to recede into the trees. Someone or something they couldn't see was pulling him away. "I spit at you!" he shouted at Marabel. He wriggled to escape from an invisible

151

grip. "I throw mud at you!" he wailed, and then disappeared into the deep, dark woods.

Silence. Even the birds seemed startled and didn't make a sound.

"What was *that*?" Ellie's voice trembled.

"I'm not sure," Marabel answered, "but I think it was a faery who did some magic to make himself look like Floriano. He must not have noticed Floriano's eyes, though— did you see?" Ellie shook her head. "Well, like I said, they were round. He was trying to get us to follow him. Faeries lure people into their world, you know, and then they make you live there for years and years that seem but a day—"

"And I suppose that once you recognized the enchantment, the spell was broken and he turned back into his regular self," Ellie said. "So where do you think the real Floriano is?"

"I don't know," Marabel answered. It was suddenly all too much for her. "I don't know any more than you do about magic or faeries or giants or anything else in this place." She sat down on a log with a thump that sent a flock of birds fluttering away, cheeping.

"I'm sorry, Ellie," she said. "It's not your fault. I'm so worried about Marco, and now Floriano's missing, and I don't know what I'm doing. . . ." She bit her lip to keep from crying.

Ellie sat down next to her and rubbed her back. "It'll be fine," she said. "Just remember we're on the same side, though, all right?"

Marabel leaned into Ellie's touch. "We should never have come," she said miserably. "We'll never find Marco, and now we've lost Floriano. I don't even know how we'll ever get home. We can't go back through the giants' mountain without risking getting caught again, so we'll have to walk around it. It's so huge, that will take days and days. And even if we do manage to free Marco, Mab's army will surely chase us all the way back to the Wall. What if we can't get through the door without Floriano? All the people and creatures in this country will be on the lookout for us." She made no effort to wipe away the tears that ran down her cheeks.

Ellie patted Marabel's hand. Marabel sighed and blew her nose on a leaf. "We should go home," she said. "My father's probably furious that I disobeyed him, and I miss my little brother and sisters."

"I miss my mother," Ellie said softly. "I hope she's not too terribly worried about me. But we can't go back now, don't you see? We've come too far. We can't give up and leave Marco, and Floriano, too. It's time someone put a stop to Mab, and it doesn't look like anyone will do it but us."

"What can the two of us do against Mab and a lot of Evils?"

Ellie stood up. "I don't know," she said, "but there's only one way to find out." She gave Marabel a hand up.

"Thanks," Marabel said. She still wasn't confident, but she owed it to Marco to keep trying. She dusted leaves and grass off her garb. "Thanks especially for reminding me of what's important. But before we go, let's look for Floriano one more time."

Together, they returned to the spot where they'd last seen the unicorn and poked around the bushes. Ellie saw what might have been hoofprints and might have been nothing, but they didn't go much of anyplace. They shouted Floriano's name, startling squirrels and birds. But nothing answered.

It grew dark, and they decided to spend the night where they were. If Floriano didn't show up, they'd have to go on without him in the morning. They managed to find some nuts and even a few handfuls of berries that still clung to the bushes despite how rapidly autumn was approaching. Ellie recognized a plant that had edible roots. The long blue roots didn't look appetizing and they had no way to cook them, but even raw they were better than nothing.

The weather the next morning didn't improve their

mood. It was gray and chilly, and when they set out, they felt a light drizzle. It was not the kind of day that would cheer them up. And knowing that it was the twelfth day of the thrennight didn't help any. Anxiety gnawed at Marabel's stomach. Would Mab launch her attack at dawn the next day, or would she wait until the evening? Even if she waited until a few minutes before 13:13—exactly a thrennight since she made her threat—would that be enough time for Marabel to reach the castle, enter it, find Marco, and somehow rescue him?

It seemed hopeless. But she was determined to try.

A few hours later, the rain stopped. Marabel climbed a tree to harvest some nuts, and threw them down to Ellie. She was about to climb down when something came crashing through the woods. The noise grew louder and seemed to be heading straight toward them.

"Run!" Marabel commanded, trying her best to slither down the tree.

"Not without you!" Ellie countered. "Can you see anything from up there?"

Marabel peered through the leaves. Something large was coming their way. She freed herself from the branches and scrambled down the trunk.

Someone called out, "Hey!"

The voice was familiar, and they paused.

Through the woods came a long, lean figure. It was the faery from the day before, and behind him was—Floriano! The unicorn did have quite a habit of turning up when he wasn't expected. He pranced along, looking as pleased with himself as if he had just conquered a kingdom.

The faery stopped in front of Marabel. "Here's your unicorn," he said. "You *have* to take him back. He's so annoying. All he does is complain and argue. We don't want—"

The girls didn't wait to hear the rest. They flew to Floriano and threw their arms around his blue neck. Marabel looked carefully into his eyes. To her relief, his pupils were the familiar star shape, only they looked suspiciously swimmy with tears.

"So you'll take him back?" the faery asked anxiously.

"Of course we will," Marabel said. "No questions asked."

The faery produced a clipboard from behind his back and handed it to her. "Sign here at the *X*," he said, pointing to the bottom of a page. It was headed "Return of Magical Being," followed by "Reason for return." Under it was a list, with checkboxes next to each entry:

☐ Unsolicited merchandise
☐ Damaged goods

☐ Doesn't look like description
☐ Wrong size/color (specify) _____
☐ Already have one
☑ Unsuitable for purpose

Marabel happily signed her name, and then initialed where the faery's long finger pointed to a line that read "All returns final. Item will not be sent back to faeryland."

"Thank goodness," the faery said as he hurried away. "Don't bother to write!" he called over his shoulder right before he vanished.

The girls turned to Floriano. "What ever made you go with him?" Ellie asked as they stroked his white mane. He curved his neck proudly, as though being kicked out of faeryland was a great accomplishment.

"It was the most beautiful thing I'd ever seen," he answered. "Something glinted in the sunlight, and when I looked at it, a blue unicorn with a white mane and a golden horn was looking back at me." The girls exchanged puzzled glances. This was a perfect description of Floriano himself. "I'd never seen anything so lovely. When you wouldn't come with me, I decided to make his acquaintance. But I couldn't get to him. He was behind a piece of glass and whenever I moved, he did, too. While I was looking, that guy—the one who brought me back—cast a spell on me." He shuddered. "He led me to a strange place. I think it must have been faeryland."

"Floriano," Marabel said, "that was a mirror. You were looking at your own reflection in a mirror."

"I was looking at my own what in a *what*?"

"It's a piece of glass with something shiny painted on the back so you can see what you look like," Marabel explained. "You've never seen one?"

Floriano rolled his eyes. "Do you think there are things like mirrors in a stable? Would donkeys really want to see what they look like?"

"But surely you've seen your reflection in water!" Ellie exclaimed.

Floriano shook his head. "That never works very well. This was much better. I always knew I was pretty, but I didn't know I was *that* pretty," he said happily. "Can I have one of those mirror things when we get home? I know the perfect spot for it in my stall!"

"He'll be impossible from now on," Ellie whispered.

Floriano's return renewed Marabel's sense of purpose, and they headed east again with fresh energy.

Soon, they saw something that made them forget how tired and hungry they were. It was a road.

12

raffic choked the tree-lined road. Marabel hung back with Ellie and Floriano, and watched the crowd go by. Just about everyone was on foot, although an occasional carriage or wagon rattled past. They didn't know if anyone was looking for them, and they especially didn't want to run into King Matthew's messenger, who would be sure to recognize Marabel and Floriano.

Marabel recognized dwarves, carrying shovels and pickaxes; a noble white stag that strode regally down the road; both fairies and faeries; a group of young wizards and witches in green uniforms who marched down the road singing about "a hundred bottles of brew on the wall, a hundred bottles of brew"; a giant with a club over his shoulder; a tank on the back of a wagon, with water sloshing out of it. A woman holding a baby peered over its top.

Marabel wondered why the woman was in the water until she passed the baby to a man next to her. Marabel saw with delight that the baby had a fish's tail, and when the woman dove into the water, her own long, scaly tail briefly flicked into the air. Marabel and Marco had once gone out on a mermaid-watching boat in the Purple Ocean but none had appeared, and ever since then she had longed to see one.

Marabel and Ellie stepped off the path to figure out what to do next.

"We're running short on time," Marabel said. "It's got to be a *lot* faster to walk on a road than fight our way through the woods. It's riskier, but I say we go by the road."

"I say we stick to the woods," Floriano said. "They'll be looking for us. What if we run into that messenger you're so worried about?"

Normally cautious, Ellie surprised them both when she said, "Let's take the road. It doesn't look like anyone's particularly keeping an eye out, and it's sure to get us there faster."

"That's settled, then," Marabel said, trying not to sound triumphant, which would hurt Floriano's delicate feelings.

They waited for a gap to open. "Come on," Marabel said. She gripped the hilt of her sword for reassurance and stepped out, followed closely by the other two.

None of them had noticed a green-and-red toad wearing a tiny crown, who hopped to one side and croaked, "Hey! Look where you're going!"

"Sorry!" said Floriano, whose hoof had barely missed the little creature.

"No harm done," the toad said. "Mind if I hitch a ride?" And without waiting for an answer, he jumped up onto the startled unicorn's back.

"Thanks," the toad said, settling in. "It's a long way to hop. Where are you headed?"

"The castle," Marabel answered shortly. To keep him from asking why, she quickly added, "And you?"

"Home to the swamp," the toad answered. "I've been away visiting relatives."

Luckily, he didn't seem to be a chatty kind of toad. That was all he said until they reached a fork in the road, with a signpost pointing in two directions. One sign said SWAMP: 500 PEBBLES and the other said CASTLE: 2,000 PEBBLES.

The toad tapped on Floriano's shoulder. "This is where I get off," he said.

Marabel lifted him down and placed him on the ground.

"Can you tell me something before you go?" she asked.

The toad nodded agreeably. "Only fair, after the free ride!"

She pointed at the signpost. "What does that mean, about pebbles?"

The toad looked at her curiously, and then at Ellie and Floriano. He sighed. "Don't they teach *anything* in schools these days?"

"Really, we want to know," Ellie said.

"A pebble is a unit of distance," the toad said. "It's how far apart you have to space your white pebbles to leave a trail so you can find your way home, if, say, your parents leave you in the woods because they're starving." He hopped about a yard. "There. That's a pebble."

"Thank you!" they called after the toad as he hopped toward the swamp.

"That would make two thousand pebbles a little more than a mile, I think," Ellie said. Their hearts lifted. After they'd traveled so far, a mile didn't sound like much. And indeed, they hadn't walked for very long when the road took a sharp turn around a hill, and when it straightened, Mab's castle came into view.

Floriano gave an excited little skip, and the girls grabbed each other's hands and squeezed. They wanted to shout for joy, but composed themselves with difficulty so they wouldn't draw attention.

Marabel knew that her aunt's castle was ancient, far older than the palace she herself had grown up in. It was made of massive blocks of dark stone, and its towers were tall and broad. Its few windows were slits designed for archers to loose their arrows through. They were far too narrow to let much light in.

And Marco was in that grim place, without a weapon or even warm clothes. Marabel wondered if he was in a dark, smelly cell, chained to a wall, with only rats for company and rotten food thrust under the door once a day. She clenched her hand around the hilt of her sword. She was ready to use it to free her brother, if necessary, even if it was only made of wood.

They climbed the green slope. The sun shone brightly, and the few people milling around glanced at them without curiosity. A group of gnomes worked busily in the garden. It wasn't the way a witch's garden ought to look, Marabel thought—it should be bedraggled and full of thorn bushes and gnarled trees. Instead, it was neat and tidy. Many-colored flowers bloomed on long stems, and dark green shrubs were trimmed into all sorts of interesting shapes—fantastical spires and globes and even a few animals.

Strange—there were no guards in sight, the moat was dry, and the drawbridge was down. Mab must not be afraid of attackers. Perhaps everyone in the kingdom—or queendom—was too afraid of her to pose a threat. They exchanged a quick glance and strode forward, trying to look as though they belonged there. They were successful—no one tried to stop them. Marabel took a deep breath when they reached the door.

Marabel spotted a wooden board, ruled into squares like a checkerboard, hanging on the door. She examined it. In each square was a small bell with a string dangling from it so they could be rung like miniature church bells. Next to each bell was a label bearing a number. A list thumbtacked next to the sign read:

RING 1 IF YOU KNOW YOUR PARTY'S EXTENSION

RING 2 IF YOU HAVE AN APPOINTMENT WITH HER
   MAJESTY'S CHANCELLOR

RING 3 IF YOU ARE MAKING A DELIVERY

RING 4 IF YOU ARE A WITCH OR A WIZARD

RING 5 IF YOU HAVE BUSINESS OF A MAGICAL NATURE

RING 6 IF YOU HAVE BUSINESS OF A NON-MAGICAL
   NATURE

. . . and so on.

None of the sixteen labels said, "Ring this one if you want to rescue your brother" or "Ring this one if you are storming the castle." In any case, Marabel didn't want to summon anyone and answer questions. She tried to open the door, and wasn't surprised to find that it was locked. She turned to Floriano and asked, "Do you mind?"

"I'm starting to feel like a locksmith," the unicorn grumbled, but he reared up and brought the tip of his horn down where the door met the wall.

The door sprang open, showing a large stone entryway. No guards here, either. Marabel felt a prickle of uneasiness. Could it really be this easy? She heard the faint sounds of people talking, and then someone laughing far away inside the castle.

"Well," she said. "Let's go in. If we act like we know what we're doing, maybe no one will stop us."

But they hadn't gotten very far when a man came hurrying up to them. "*There* you are!" he barked. "Why are you so late? I didn't even hear you ring!"

"W-w-we didn't know which bell to—" Marabel stammered.

"Never mind now," he said impatiently. "The important thing is that you're here. Her Majesty is waiting for you."

"Her Majesty?" Marabel asked.

"Waiting for us?" Ellie squeaked.

"Of course. If you're going to be tonight's dinner entertainment, she has to hear you first and make sure you sing as well as the reports have said. She sees to everything like that herself."

"But—" Marabel started.

"You're not going to quibble over the price, are you?" the man asked. "Your agent drove a very hard bargain, and Her Majesty won't pay a penny over what was agreed on!"

"Oh, no, the price is fine," Marabel said.

"Well, then, what is it?"

"We've had a long, dry walk," Floriano put in. "We have to save our voices. You don't want us to croak like frogs when the time comes to entertain, do you?"

"What I want doesn't matter. It's what Her Majesty requires, and she requires that you sing for her and prove your skill. Come along now."

The last thing Marabel wanted to do was come face-to-face with her aunt—she just wanted to find Marco and get out as quickly as possible. She didn't know how well Mab had seen her during Marco's kidnapping, and she didn't want to risk being recognized. But they had no choice.

They hurried down the long corridor, lined with suits of

armor, tapestries, and heavy wooden furniture that looked like no one had used it in centuries. The man threw open a door and ushered them in.

Marabel, expecting a coldly elegant formal chamber, was surprised at the homey little room. It was filled with soft-looking, rather shabby armchairs, small tables piled with books and other objects, a few musical instruments scattered around, and portraits hanging on every wall. Two shaggy white dogs jumped up from a rug in front of the fireplace and ran to them, their tails wagging.

A woman was seated at a desk, her back to the door. Marabel knew it had to be her aunt Mab. She looked down, hoping to escape notice.

"The singers for this evening, Your Majesty," the man said.

Mab rose and faced them. "Well?"

"Well, what?" asked Floriano.

"Well, let's hear you sing," Mab said.

"We have to save our voices for tonight," Ellie said nervously.

Floriano shot a warning look at the girls and mouthed, "Hush," at them. "I'll sing a solo," he said more loudly. "Their voices aren't as robust as mine." Marabel started to object but Floriano shot her an even fiercer look, and she didn't say anything. She closed her eyes and cringed inwardly. What would a unicorn's voice sound like? As soon as he neighed, Mab would know for sure that they were impostors.

Then Floriano opened his mouth. To Marabel's astonishment, he didn't neigh, but sang in a beautiful, rich tenor. Ellie stared at him with her mouth hanging open, and Marabel realized that she was doing the same thing.

Marabel snapped her mouth shut as Floriano finished. The unicorn bowed, extending one foreleg and lowering his head.

Silence fell. Then Mab said, "Even if the two girls caw like ravens, you're hired. All of you."

"I wouldn't perform with anyone who cawed," Floriano said stiffly. "It would ruin my reputation."

The queen turned to her manservant. "Balthazar, take them to the green room to rest and have some refreshments. I want them to perform both before and during the dinner. Have the scientists and generals arrived?"

"Not all of them, Your Majesty," the man—Balthazar—said. "The Minister for the Management of Magic is delayed, and the census taker has sent his report on ahead. He asked me to tell you that more instances of misbehavior have been—"

"Enough," Mab snapped. "Never speak of classified material in public!"

"A thousand pardons," Balthazar said. He looked at Marabel and the others as though he'd forgotten they were there, and opened the door. He motioned them out.

Marabel relaxed a little. Her aunt had barely glanced at her. The first hurdle they faced in the castle was behind them. She thought she would burst out of her skin with impatience as she turned toward the door.

But before they could leave, the queen said, "Young ladies, I see you're not carrying any bags. Do you not have something more festive to change into for your performance? What you're wearing is tattered and filthy—hardly stage apparel!"

Marabel wanted to retort, "You try walking for twelve days and see how clean you'd be," but she kept her mouth shut. Ellie muttered something about losing their luggage, and something else about giants and a man-wolf.

"Well, we can't have you going in front of my guests dressed like that," Mab said. "I'll tell my wardrobe mistress to find you something. Come here and let me look at you."

Marabel didn't know what to do except turn back and join Ellie in front of her aunt.

Mab looked Ellie up and down. "Pretty, in a conventional sort of way." Then she turned to Marabel, who felt her face turn hot. Mab started to say something and stopped. After a moment, she asked, "Have we met before?"

"No, Your Majesty," Marabel mumbled.

"Odd." Mab stared at her. Marabel felt more and more uncomfortable. "I feel sure . . . You look so familiar."

"I would remember if I had met Your Majesty," Marabel said.

"So you would." Her aunt's voice regained its brisk tone. "Well, you must need to rest and rehearse. I'll have the wardrobe mistress bring you some things. Balthazar, take them away."

The man beckoned, and they hurried after him.

All the way to the door, Marabel felt her aunt's eyes boring into her back.

13

Balthazar led them up a flight of stairs and then down one corridor after another until Marabel was thoroughly confused. He finally opened a door and motioned them in. "The green room," he said. "You can wait here until the wardrobe mistress has found something suitable for you to wear."

All the furniture in the room was upholstered in forest green, the floor was paved with sea-green tile, the walls were painted a lime shade, and the curtains were the fresh color of spring leaves. The curtains turned even the sunlight green.

"We need to rest," Marabel told him. "Please have the wardrobe mistress leave the clothes outside the door and not disturb us."

"As you wish." He hurried away.

"We have to look for Marco right now," Marabel said. "I can't stand waiting another minute. I don't want them to come by with costumes and find us gone. Come on."

The door wasn't locked. Marabel cracked it open and peered first one way down the hall, and then the other. "Let's go," she whispered. She looked back. Ellie was right behind her, but Floriano hovered inside the room. "What are you *doing*?" Marabel asked in a low voice. "We don't have much time!"

Floriano tossed his head. "I'm here for the adventure," he said. "Not to rescue anyone. And the adventure I've always wanted was to become a star. I heard some stable hands talking once about something called *Magikos Has Talent*, and ever since then I've known that becoming a star was the life for me. Just think what it would do for my career if I performed for a queen!"

The girls tried to change his mind, but Floriano was determined. "This is my chance," he kept repeating. "You go on and do what you have to do. When they come back, I'll make up an excuse for you. Stage fright or something."

Marabel couldn't spare any more time. So, with a quick good-bye and one backward glance, she rejoined Ellie and they set off in search of the dungeon. Marabel tried to tell herself they didn't need him, but she knew she was going to miss the conceited unicorn.

The castle was quiet and dim, and it smelled musty. Every once in a while they passed a sign that read HERE BE THE WAY OUT in large red letters with another, smaller sign below it that added DON'T FORGET TO VISIT OUR GIFT SHOP BEFORE YOU LEAVE!

Their footsteps echoed in the empty hallways, and Marabel grew more and more anxious that they would never find the dungeon. Marabel was sure they'd be wandering the corridors forever when they stumbled on a floor plan of the castle hanging on a wall. A red dot in the middle of the plan was marked YOU BE HERE.

"Aha!" Ellie said. "Now where is the dungeon?"

"Let's see," Marabel muttered. "If we just passed the keep, and the postern is on our left—"

A door in front of them suddenly swung open, and a tall female figure, clothed in a black robe, stepped out and looked straight at them.

"You there!" she called out.

It was a witch. She wasn't carrying a broom or wearing a

high-pointed hat, but such a strong air of magic and authority hovered around her that they just knew. "Where are you supposed to be?" the witch demanded.

"Well—" Ellie said.

"The green room," Marabel managed.

"And who gave you permission to leave it?"

They had no answer, so neither one said anything.

"Let me see your passes," she said.

They looked at each other. Ellie made a show of rummaging in her pouch and then in her hood. "Must have lost them," she mumbled. "You don't have them, uh, Aurora, do you?"

Aurora? Marabel was puzzled for an instant, then caught on that Ellie was hiding her identity. "No," she said. "I thought *you* had them."

"I gave them to you!" Ellie said.

"No, you didn't." Marabel wondered how long they'd be able to keep this up.

"Is there some trouble here?" broke in another voice, and Floriano trotted toward them. "Where are you girls supposed to be?" he demanded.

"What do—" Marabel started, but the unicorn shot her a meaningful glare, and she stopped.

"That's what I was trying to find out," the witch said. "And who are *you*?"

"Her Majesty's new head of security," he rattled out. "I'll take these two with me. When I report their capture, I'll recommend a commendation for your diligence. Come along, you two." He nudged the stunned girls around the corner.

"That was quick thinking!" Marabel said once they were out of earshot. She patted Floriano at the base of his horn. "Thanks."

"Why did you leave the green room? What happened to singing for the queen?" Ellie asked.

Floriano shrugged. "I realized that wasn't much of an adventure. It's more adventurous to go on a quest. Besides, I can try out for *Magikos Has Talent* after we get home."

"Oh, come on," Marabel said. "Admit it. You missed us."

Floriano snorted without answering.

Marabel had lost track of where they were. She stopped, and spotted yet another HERE BE THE WAY OUT sign. It gave her an idea, and she stopped walking to think.

"What?" Floriano asked.

"The numbers on the plan started in the basement, right? And the dungeon was number two or three or something, wasn't it? That would mean the dungeon's in the lowest part of the castle."

Ellie nodded. "They always are. That's why they're cold and damp."

Marabel said eagerly, "So let's see if one of the stairways goes past the exit at ground level and on to the basement. That's where the dungeon must be."

They tried a few doors unsuccessfully. Finally, Marabel spotted a door tucked into a corner. She opened it, expecting to be disappointed yet again, but instead, it opened on a broad stairway with a ramp along its side. Surely this led to the dungeon!

Calling, "Wait here!" she went down one flight, and was thrilled to see that there were more stairs. The second flight down was so long that she was starting to think it was some kind of magical staircase to nowhere, when she turned a corner and almost ran into another door. This one was marked AUTHORIZED PERSONNEL ONLY. DOOR IS ALARMED.

Plague it, Marabel thought as she trudged up the stairs again and told the others what she had found.

"Well, that's no good, then. If there's an alarm on the door, they'd find us as soon as we opened it, wouldn't they?" Ellie said.

Marabel looked at Floriano. "Is there something about that door-opening magic in your horn that would keep an alarm from sounding?"

He shook his head. "'Fraid not. It only opens things. Nothing about turning off alarms."

"Let's take a closer look at the door," Ellie suggested. "Maybe we can open it only partway or really slowly, and the alarm won't go off."

Ellie and Marabel went down the stairs, and Floriano took the ramp. They stopped and faced the alarmed door. Floriano peered at it in the semidark, brushing it with his horn.

A sudden "Eek!" made them all jump back.

They looked at one another. "Who said that?" Ellie asked.

"Not me," Floriano and Marabel chorused.

"It was me," said an unfamiliar voice.

They looked up, down, into the corners, back up the stairway—nothing.

"Where are you?" Marabel asked.

"Right in front of your nose," said the voice. "But don't hurt me! I'm just a simple door. I wouldn't hurt *you*!"

"Don't be alarmed—" Marabel stopped short as she realized what she had said. "Wait, are you *alarmed* as in 'frightened'?"

"I can't help it," the door whimpered. "It's so dark in here, and there are spiders and crickets, and I swear there's a ghost that comes out at night carrying its own head, and—"

"It's all right," Ellie said soothingly. She raised her hand slowly and stroked the door. It appeared to flinch. "We won't hurt you. We only want to go through and find the dungeon."

"The *dungeon*!" the door squawked. "Why, that's the most terrifying part of the whole castle!"

"We know," Marabel said, "but that's what we want to do. If we open the door, will you keep quiet and not give us away?"

"I'll try," the voice said with a quaver. "But be quick. If you leave me open for long, who knows what will come through? I may scream!"

Marabel turned the knob. They slipped through and then closed the door behind them. "Thank you," Marabel said.

They looked down the windowless, silent hallway, dimly lit by torches. It smelled of mold and of musty air that never moved, and the walls felt cold and slick.

Ellie's icy fingers clutched Marabel's.

"I don't like this place," Floriano said, barely above a whisper. "Let's go back."

"It's all right," Marabel said. "It's just old and empty. Nothing to be afraid of." But despite her words, her heart raced. They couldn't turn back, not when they were so close. Not when the thrennight would be up in a few hours, if they were lucky. She wanted to call out to her brother, but didn't dare—who knew what guards she would summon, what strange beings she would awaken?

They proceeded down the dingy hall, their feet stirring up dust. They stopped in front of a huge door.

"This must be it," she said.

"Duh," Floriano said. He gestured upward with one golden hoof at a sign that said DUNGEON.

Unlike the door in the giants' home, this one had a smaller door cut into it. Its handle was at regular height, and it opened smoothly.

Dim as the hallway was, the chamber behind the door was even darker. So dark, in fact, that when Marabel took a tentative step in, she didn't realize that something was in there until it was too late. She smacked into a cold, hard surface. It seemed to curve slightly away from her, and it seemed to be—yes, it was moving.

She leaped back, knocking Ellie off her feet. The two of them got tangled up in Floriano's long legs. Then came a sickening sound: the slam of the door behind them.

Paralyzed by fear and the pitch dark, they clung together. Floriano whimpered and the girls shuddered.

A light flashed and a flame flew above their heads. It landed on the head of a torch on the wall, and illuminated something large that shifted and moved sinuously, like a giant snake.

Two glowing eyes glared at them, and then a huge mouth

opened, showing gleaming, yellowish teeth, each as long as a human forearm. A puff of smoke came out of a mouth that grinned without humor, and realization struck them all at the same time: They were staring at the scaly face of a dragon.

14

The dragon was curled up, as dragons usually are, on a pile of treasure. Gold, silver, and brilliant gems winked and twinkled coldly in the wavering light of the torch. As Marabel's eyes got used to the semidarkness, she made out the dragon's orange scales, as large as dinner plates. He was even bigger than the one Mab had left to guard the Magikian palace. In fact, he was so huge that he scraped his head against the ceiling whenever he moved. The dragon had evidently been bumping his head for a long time; the scales on his scalp had been pushed forward over his tiny eyes, giving him a malevolent glare.

The dragon yawned, showing his long and pointed teeth and a surprisingly pink tongue curling up at the end like a cat's. "Who the heck are you?" he asked. "How did you get in here?"

"We're ... we're nobody," Marabel managed to squeak out. "We got lost. We're sorry to bother you. We'll leave now."

"I don't think so." The dragon slid his tail in front of the door. Ellie looked sick, and Marabel didn't feel much better. "I don't think you're lost. No one comes down here by accident. Everyone in the queendom knows that the dungeon is in the bottom of the castle, and that the dungeon is guarded by Hotshot. That's me, folks. Hotshot."

"Really, Mr. Hotshot, we didn't know any of that," Floriano said. "We're new to the neighborhood, and we've never heard of the dungeon or of you."

"Incredible." The dragon shook his head in disgust, his wide mouth turning down even more. "I'm famous. Everyone knows about Hotshot except you losers. Everyone also knows about dragons, and how we guard treasures and dungeons. We're amazing, to be perfectly honest."

"We don't know anything about dragons," Ellie said

earnestly. "We come from . . . from a place that doesn't have many dragons. We only know what we hear in tales."

"Unbelievable. So if you know about us from tales, I bet you think you know what's going to happen now."

Marabel shook her head, unable to speak. Her tongue seemed to be stuck to the roof of her mouth.

The dragon went on, "I bet you think that I'm going to turn out to be a nice dragon, a sweet dragon who's sad that everyone's afraid of him, because he just wants to be *friends*." The last word was uttered with a sneer that made Marabel's toes curl.

Marabel *had* been hoping that the situation would turn out to be something like that. After all, despite everything she'd ever heard about giants and ogres, the giant family hadn't wanted to eat them, and the troll had let them over the bridge, and Cornelius had been friendly, even though he was an ogre. She had hoped that maybe dragons, too, were less fierce than their reputation suggested.

She managed to croak, "It doesn't matter to us whether you want to be friends."

"Good." Hotshot stretched one long front leg out as far as he could in his cramped quarters, and yawned until Marabel could see embers glowing at the back of his throat. "Because there's no such thing as a friendly dragon. Believe me, we're generally known to be *un*friendly. You might even say fierce. It's incredible, really incredible, ⸬ w fierce we can be." He puffed out a thin stream of fire, and they flinched.

"What are you going to do with us?" Ellie quavered. Marabel wondered whether she was more afraid of being eaten by a dragon or of being squeezed into this tiny room.

"That's something you should have thought of before you came down here." Hotshot shook his head, and smoke puffed out his nostrils. "Some people. Losers."

"Wait a second," Marabel broke in. What had the dragon said earlier? "Did you say that you guard the dungeon?"

"My friend, Hotshot is the best dungeon guard in the queendom, okay? Unbelievable. Just unbelievable."

"All right, fine, you're the best dungeon guard in the queendom," Marabel said. "So where is it?"

"The dungeon? It's right there." He gestured to one side with a front foot, which was fringed with wicked-looking claws.

"Are there any prisoners in it right now?" she asked.

He looked at her sharply. "Who are you anyway? Why do you care who's in the dungeon?"

"Official business," Floriano said uncertainly. "We've been sent to make sure they're being treated humanely."

"Oh, nice! Humanely? Why should they be treated

humanely? Criminals, all of them. The queen should toss those losers off the tower, like they did in the old days. That's the only way to keep the homeland secure. I'm tired of the way criminals are coddled nowadays. It's not good for the queendom, and it's not good for the law-abiding citizens, believe me."

"Can we go in and see him—I mean, see *them*, please, sir?" Marabel dropped her best princess curtsey, hoping that her etiquette lessons would finally be useful.

The dragon narrowed his already narrow eyes. "Why should I let you in? Who sent you anyway? Something isn't right here."

"Maybe we should go away for now." Ellie inched toward the door, ignoring the fact that it was still blocked by the dragon's long orange tail. "We'll get the, um, paperwork done and come back tomorrow. Come on, Marabel." Too late, Ellie clapped her hand over her mouth.

"Marabel?" The dragon shot up and bumped into the ceiling. "Ow!" He rubbed his head with a clawed foot and cursed dragon curses. "I think someone is looking for you, *Marabel*," he said with a smirk, stretching his thin lips back almost to his pointed ears. He punched a claw into a red button on the wall in front of him, and a hideous racket of bells and sirens broke out.

It was hard to believe that the room could hold even one more person, but in less time than they would have thought possible, Marabel, Ellie, and Floriano were surrounded by soldiers.

The soldiers weren't human, however. They were small, with brownish teeth and bulging eyes. And they were purple—not a pretty violet color, but a muddy, blueish purple. Goblins! Were goblins good or bad? Marabel couldn't remember, but from the way they were pointing spears and swords at her and her friends, the situation didn't look hopeful.

"Make way for the queen!" barked the goblin who appeared to be in charge.

Mab strode in, accompanied by her wizard, Veneficus. "This had better not be another false alarm, Hotshot," she said.

"I'm a huge admirer of Your Majesty," the dragon said. "Huge. But even you can make a mistake once in a while. I already know what you're going to say when you see what I've accomplished, you mark my words. You're going to say I'm a guy who can handle things. You're going to say I'm the greatest dungeon guard you've ever seen. Just take a look over there, and tell me what you see. Go on. Tell me."

Mab swung around to where Floriano and the girls were huddled. "My musicians!" she said. "What are you doing down here?"

"That's where you're wrong, Your Majesty." Hotshot sounded so smug that Marabel wished she could slap him. "Not musicians. I'm not surprised you couldn't tell. You don't have the experience that I have. I've seen lots of musicians, my friend, and these aren't—"

"Oh, stop it," Mab said. To Marabel's surprise, he did stop, but he looked indignant, and another little puff of smoke escaped his nostrils.

Mab looked at them more closely, and then a slow smile spread across her face. "I *thought* you looked familiar," she said to Marabel. "I know you now. You're my niece, aren't you?"

Marabel stuck her chin out. She saw no point in trying to hide her identity any longer, and she refused to lie or beg for mercy. "Yes," she said, relieved that her voice didn't tremble. "I'm Princess Marabel. I've come for my brother."

Her aunt burst out laughing. "And you think I'll just hand him over? You made a grave error in coming here, missy. Now I have *two* royal hostages, not one!"

"It might as well be only one," Marabel said. "My parents don't care what happens to me. If you have Marco, that's all that matters. He's the Chosen One. He's the one who's supposed to save the kingdom. Don't count on them doing anything to rescue me."

"Oh, boo-hoo," Mab said. "Poor little neglected princess—everyone pays attention to your brother and not to you, is that right? Don't come to me for sympathy—I've had to fight the same battle my whole life, and look at me now!" She swung her arm around, indicating the chamber, the treasure, the dragon. "It's all mine!"

Veneficus was getting impatient. "Find out how they got here," he put in. "They had to have had some help."

"Well?" the queen demanded. "Did my brother send you? He didn't give you much of an entourage!"

"Nobody knows we're here," Marabel said. "It's just the three of us. We've made it on foot from Magikos." Her voice trembled and she cleared her throat. "We've come to rescue Marco."

"*You?*" Her aunt sounded surprised, but not mocking, and Marabel was emboldened to go on.

"Nobody else was coming to save Marco. My father thinks he's going to free himself. Symposia, the head priestess—"

"I know who Symposia is," Mab said drily. "Let me

guess—she said to consult the Book, and the Book said exactly what your father wanted it to say."

What was her aunt implying? It sounded like something Cornelius had said: "Perhaps the priests read only what they wish to see in it."

She didn't have time to wonder about that now. "I don't know, Aunt Mab, and I don't care! All I know is that nobody was going to try to help Marco, so I had to do it. And Ellie and Floriano came, too."

Mab's eyes softened. "Well, I must say I'm surprised," she said. "Who would have thought that Matthew's child would have the... But of course, you're Marianna's daughter as well." For a moment she smiled and looked lost in thought. Then her face hardened again. "Now my brother will have no choice but to do what's right! The thrennight is almost up. There's still time for me to punish you for trespassing and for attempted freeing of a prisoner, though. You are all confined to the dungeon, and while there you must..." Mab paused, as though trying to think of a punishment severe enough for them. Marabel trembled at the thought of what that might be.

Finally, Mab said in obvious exasperation, "Oh, I don't know! You must each write one thousand times: 'I will not storm the castle.' There! That ought to keep you out of trouble until I think of something that will really teach you a lesson."

Marabel couldn't help wondering why her aunt was letting them off so easily. Mab was probably trying to get Marabel to drop her guard so that she'd be unprepared for a more awful punishment later on. She made up her mind to be vigilant.

Mab turned to the soldiers. "Guards! Throw them in the dungeon. Don't let them out until I give the order."

"No!" Ellie wailed. "Please, please don't lock us up! I can't stand it!"

Marabel grabbed Ellie's hand, wishing she could comfort her, and desperately asked her aunt, "Why won't you let Marco go? What did he ever do to you?"

"Nothing," Mab said. "Neither have you. You have the bad luck to be mere pawns in the game that your father and I are playing—the game we've played since we were children. Guards! Do as I say! In the dungeon with them!"

Marabel cried out as goblin soldiers seized her and Ellie by the arms, and Floriano by the horn. The unicorn whinnied and reared, but the soldiers expertly dodged his hooves.

The last thing Marabel heard before the dungeon door slammed shut was her aunt's mocking laughter.

Ellie began to sob, "Let me out! Open the door! Please,

please let me out!" Ellie pounded and pounded on the door. No answer.

Marabel looked for a window, another door, anything that would help Ellie calm down, but all she could see was Marco.

Marco!

15

arco stared at them in shock. He slowly rose to his feet. Her twin, her best friend, her ally. Despite her worst fears, he wasn't shackled to a wall or confined in a tiny cage. Instead, he was sitting on a long, low sofa. On a table in front of him was what looked like a bowl of cereal and a tall glass of bluefruit juice.

Marabel took a step toward him.

"*Mara?*" he said in a dazed voice.

She ran across the room and flung herself at her brother. They hugged each other until they could hardly breathe, laughing and crying at the same time. They both babbled, asking questions, not pausing long enough to answer. Marco kept saying, "I can't believe it! I can't believe you're here!"

When they finally calmed down, Marabel said, "I can't believe it, either—we made it! And you're fine! I've been so worried."

Marco sat back down on the sofa and patted the cushion next to him. Marabel sat, staring at his face as though afraid that if she took her eyes off him, he would disappear. "I'm sorry you were worried," Marco said. "I've been worried about you, too. Nobody would tell me what was going on in Magikos."

"What you'd expect, I suppose. They had a Ritual, and Symposia said you didn't need any help."

Marco asked, "What are you doing here, then? Did Aunt Mab kidnap you, too?"

"Um," Marabel answered, "I'm rescuing you."

He looked pointedly at the locked door, and they both burst out laughing. Marabel couldn't help it; the situation was so absurd and so hopeless, nothing was left to do but laugh.

"We came so close," Marabel said, suddenly serious. "We made it all the way here. And, Marco, I've been so worried that she was hurting you."

"Hurting me? No, not at all. It's actually pretty nice in here, except for a fire-breathing dragon outside the door. There's lots of food and there's even WizFi, plus books and music and things."

Marabel told Marco everything that had happened, starting with the hidden tunnel. As she relayed the story to her brother, she suddenly realized how much she had learned in a thrennight.

"What made you come up with the idea of hitting the man-wolf with that old practice sword?" Marco asked. "I'm surprised it didn't break!"

"I had to do *something*, and the sword was right there," Marabel confessed.

"I wouldn't have been brave enough to do that." Marco sounded impressed. "I'd be afraid that hitting him would make him mad. I'd have tried to convince him to leave us alone."

That was so Marco! He always did his best to be reasonable, while Marabel tended to go the direct route. But then Marabel remembered the man-wolf's long teeth and the cold glint in his eye, and she didn't think even Marco would have been able to do much convincing.

"How did you figure out how to answer the riddle?" Marco asked when Marabel told him about the bridge troll.

"I was pretty desperate, I guess, and after Ellie and Floriano gave him answers he wasn't expecting, it just came to me. Oh, and wait until you hear about the faery!"

She ended her tale by telling him about their encounter with Hotshot. Marco rolled his eyes at the mention of the dragon.

"He's such a jerk," Marco said. "He's cranky from being all cramped in there, but that's no reason for him to act the way he does. He says when he first moved here, he was much smaller and his lair was more comfortable. I bet that's only an excuse, though. I bet he was just as much of a jerk then."

Marabel had bigger questions. "Is Mab still threatening to have her wizard turn you into a frog?" The idea was so appalling!

"That's what she says. Or a snake, if Veneficus can figure out how to do it. You, too, now, I guess."

"We have to get out of here," Marabel said. "We can't let that happen."

"Do you think I haven't tried? The door is locked, there's a huge dragon on the other side of it—"

Ellie said, "And there's a witch, too, and there's that Veneficus guy and who knows who else."

"—and goblin soldiers all over. It's no use, Marabel. Either Father does what Mab wants, or we're going to wind up as two frogs in a terrarium. Or the moat, if we're lucky. At least we'd have a little more room there."

"A dragon and a witch might not be as hard to get past as you think. We've made it past trolls, giants, and an ogre—well, the ogre turned out not to be a problem, actually."

"But the others were!" Marco said. "And you got past all of them."

Marabel wanted to be humble, but she couldn't help swelling with pride at his words.

"We all worked together," she said. "And maybe we could fight a dragon."

"Fight a dragon?" asked Marco, disbelieving. "No way. Besides, we don't have any weapons. Unless you count that." He nodded at the wooden practice sword still hanging from Marabel's belt.

Marabel rested her hand on the sword's hilt. "Hmm," she said. "How about if we try to trick Hotshot? Tell him we have some magic charms or potions or something."

Marco shook his head. "He wouldn't fall for that. If you had a charm, you'd have used it on Aunt Mab or the goblins."

"Let's try talking to him," Ellie suggested.

"You're right," Marabel said. "Wait till you see this, Marco!" She turned to the unicorn and said, "Go ahead."

Floriano reared up. Marco gasped as Floriano's horn

glowed and touched the latch. But to Marabel's dismay, the door stayed shut.

"What was that?" Marco asked. "I don't get it."

"Usually Floriano can unlock doors with his horn. But maybe it's stuck," Ellie said. "You saw how hard the soldier had to kick it to get it open."

Marabel tried the handle, but the door didn't budge.

"Huh," she said, puzzled. "It's still locked. Try again, Floriano."

But before the unicorn could comply, his horn beeped, and bright letters appeared on his forehead. "Wait a second," Marabel said. "Lower your head." She read the words that circled the base of Floriano's horn: "'Attempt failed. Requires update to UniHorn version 13.0.1.'"

"Oh no," Marco groaned.

"It's all right," Floriano assured him. "I have a UniHorn account, so I can update as soon as we're logged on to the WizFi."

They all attempted to figure out Mab's WizFi password, punching letters and numbers on the keypad on Floriano's forehead. Nothing worked, and they grew more and more frustrated. The clock was ticking—Marabel just *had* to do something, and fast!

It wasn't going to work. They had to come up with

something else. A rescue was unlikely and a war was coming. How had everything gone wrong so quickly? And what would happen if her father's army attacked? They couldn't just sit there until Veneficus came and turned them into frogs! She shuddered.

"Cheer up," Marco said. "It's almost lunchtime. We can think more clearly after we've eaten." A blinding bright green light flashed as three plates of sandwiches appeared on the table. On the floor sat a bucket of oats.

Floriano trotted over and buried his nose in the bucket. "Mmm," he said. "Warm."

Marabel picked up a sandwich—her favorite, grilled cheese—and was about to bite into it when Ellie stopped her. "Bewitched food?" she asked. "Are you seriously going to eat that?"

"I've been eating it for twelve days," Marco said. "Hasn't hurt me yet."

"If we don't eat, we'll starve." Marabel took a bite. "Doesn't taste magical."

Ellie gave in and they ate until the plates were empty.

As she wiped her mouth with a linen napkin, Marabel was struck by an uneasy thought. Was the witch fattening Marco up with all this food? Was she planning to *eat* him?

She'd heard of witches eating people, especially children. Her brother did look a little pudgy, now that she examined him.

Ellie sighed. "If we can't unlock the door or log on to the WizFi, what are we going to do?"

"Whatever we do, it has to wait until after the guard comes by," Marco said. "He checks on me every day."

"A guard! Why didn't you say so?" Marabel exclaimed. "Maybe we can outsmart him!"

"Possibly," Marco said. "He's a pretty nice guy, actually, but I don't know how easy he'd be to fool. He should be here in about an hour. In the meantime, there's a bathroom in there." He pointed at a door in the far wall. "Excuse me for saying so, but the two of you could use a bath."

The bathroom held two enormous tubs, and the girls scrubbed themselves, rinsed, and then scrubbed again. The hot water eased Marabel's worries a little. She helped Ellie squeeze water out of her thick hair, and smiled to herself. Only a thrennight before, it had been Ellie helping *her* to wash her hair. Now it seemed perfectly natural to be the one helping. It felt nice.

They discarded their filthy garbs. Marabel chose a fawn-colored tunic, fringed on the bottom, and matching trousers. Ellie chose a blue outfit. The cloth was warm and very soft, but it was odd to put on something different than a garb, and the lack of a hooded tunic made them feel almost naked.

They combed each other's damp hair and rejoined Marco in the outer room, where he was still sitting on the sofa.

"No guard?" Marabel asked.

"Not yet," Marco said.

Marabel groaned.

"Here." Marco handed Marabel a small box. "This will help pass the time."

The box was made of shiny metal. Two handles stuck out on either side, and jeweled buttons were arranged in rows on the front. They were marked with symbols—a ruby triangle pointing left, a diamond triangle pointing right, an outline of a square in what looked like sapphires, and other simple shapes. "What is it?"

"I'll show you." He pointed the box at a shiny black rectangle hanging on the opposite wall and pressed one of the buttons.

"Whoa!" Marabel recoiled. The rectangle had lit up, showing a flat stage, with tiny creatures of all sorts—humans, dragons, trolls, ogres, manticores, dwarves, giants, and more—running around aimlessly.

"It's a game," Marco explained. "Those are the imps who

live in that place. They like to play—that's all they ever want to do. Here, let me show you."

Marabel learned a game called *Queen's Quest*, and then Marco showed her how to play *MagicCraft III* and *Angry Phoenixes*. She got so caught up in aiming slingshots loaded with phoenixes at wild boars that were, for some reason, sitting in trees, that she almost forgot that the thrennight was almost up, that a dragon was keeping them confined, and even that she and Marco were likely going to be turned into cold-blooded animals.

After a while, Marco looked at the door. "It's strange he's not here yet," he said. "I hope he isn't sick or anything. We're kind of friends. He's not much older than us, and he sometimes plays *Impcraft* with me. He talks to me about the castle and what's going on, like Aunt Mab's meeting tonight with the people trying to figure out how to solve that magical creature problem they're having here."

"What kind of problem?" Marabel asked.

"Does that matter?" Floriano broke in. "Shouldn't we be trying to figure out how to get out of here?"

"Wait," Ellie said. "Aren't you the Chosen One, Marco? Shouldn't you be the one coming up with the answers?"

Marco looked embarrassed. "I've tried and tried," he said. "I don't know what to do."

"The Book doesn't say that he has to figure out what to do," Marabel said. "Just that he has to *do* it, whatever it is. My father has advisers and all sorts of people to give him advice. Maybe we're the advisers to the Chosen One."

"Can we convince Hotshot to let us go?" asked Ellie.

Marco shook his head. "Why would he do that? What would we be able to offer him in exchange for our freedom? He doesn't care about anything but himself."

"Let's think," Marabel said. "He has all the treasure that could possibly fit in that room, right? What else do dragons want, aside from gold and jewels?"

"The only thing other than treasure that I've ever heard of dragons wanting," Marco said slowly, "is . . . never mind."

"What?" Marabel asked.

"The only thing they seem to want," Marco said reluctantly, "you know, when they're rampaging through the countryside and eating all the farmers' sheep and burning things down and all—"

"Right, behaving like dragons," Marabel said.

"Well, what do they always ask for in exchange for not doing those things anymore?"

"Oh," Ellie said after a moment.

"Oh, right," said Marabel.

"What?" Floriano asked. "What is it they ask for?"

"They always ask," Marco said reluctantly, "for a maiden. To eat. Usually a princess."

"Does Mab actually give Hotshot people to eat?" Floriano was horrified.

"I don't think so. If he'd eaten a maiden I think I would have heard something."

They all shuddered at the thought of what that would sound like.

"So is this your plan?" Ellie asked him. "To offer your sister to a dragon?"

"What? No!" Marco sounded shocked. "Never!"

"So what *does* Hotshot eat?" Floriano asked.

"I don't think he eats anything," Marco said. "He's squeezed so tight that he might be afraid he'll grow if he keeps eating, and then he'll have to move to someplace bigger. Dragons are like hermit crabs—they need to find a new home every time they grow."

They were silent. Then Marabel stood up.

"All right," she said. "We'll tell him he can . . ." She swallowed. "He can eat me if he'll let the rest of you go."

"That's not going to happen," Marco said firmly.

"There's nothing else to do. Just . . ." Marabel took a deep breath. "Just say good-bye to everyone for me, all right? Father and Maggie and the little ones—"

She froze. Something had occurred to her, exactly when she wasn't trying to come up with a solution. It was crazy, and it probably wouldn't work—but it was something.

"Wait a second," she said slowly, trying not to extinguish the tiny spark of her idea. "I've thought of something. Listen." The others gathered close while she laid out her plan. They conferred in whispers until they had agreed on all the steps.

"I don't know," Marco said. "Hotshot'll never admit that anything of his isn't the best, even if it's obviously true."

"We have to try," Marabel said. Her plan didn't stand much chance of working, but anything was better than sitting around doing nothing. She took a deep breath. "Ellie, you're on!"

16

Ellie swallowed and spoke into the crack at the edge of the door. "Oh, Mr. Hotshot!" she called in her sweetest voice.

No answer.

"Can we talk with you, Mr. Hotshot?"

They heard clanking and banging as the dragon moved. "What do you want?" came a surly voice. "I was counting my silver shields, and you made me lose my place. Now I have to start all over again."

"We have a proposition for you," Marco said. "Can you let us out for a minute so we can discuss it?"

"You people are crazy," the dragon said, and a little flame flickered in under the door. Ellie jumped back. Hotshot went on, "There's no proposition you losers can make that would interest me. Be quiet and let me count."

"Hush and listen," Marabel said. "Can you hear us through the door?"

"Are you kidding? My hearing is excellent. It's the best. It's—"

"What we want to talk about," Marabel said, "is that you seem awfully confined in that room."

"What do you mean?" He sounded indignant. "This place is huge! It's enormous! So luxurious! It's Hotshot's home, and believe me, Hotshot wouldn't live in anything but the best."

"See?" Marco whispered.

Marabel ignored him and said, "You've outgrown it."

"You keep bumping your head," Ellie pointed out.

"You can't even straighten your tail," Marco added.

"Worst of all, you're locked in," Marabel said. "How can you stand it?"

"You're a magical being," Floriano said. "You deserve better. You shouldn't be locked up like a . . . like a stupid donkey. You should have your own wild place to live in, where you can come and go whenever you want, and not take orders from anyone."

The dragon was silent.

"Hello?" Marabel called tentatively.

"So what are you suggesting?" the dragon asked, his bluster gone, at least for the moment.

They exchanged looks, hardly daring to hope. Marabel took another deep breath.

"Not far from here there's a big cave. It's easily twice the size of this room. We spent the night there at the beginning of our journey, and it was very comfortable. It has a nice view, and a stream nearby."

More silence. Then, "Private entrance?" Hotshot asked.

"Absolutely," Marabel assured him. "And plenty big enough for you."

"Noisy neighbors?"

"No neighbors, except a few birds and squirrels."

"Open-concept floor plan?"

Marabel wasn't sure what this meant, but it sounded like Hotshot didn't want the cave to have a lot of small rooms, so she said, "Very open."

"New appliances?"

What would a dragon want with appliances? "No, there are no appliances. That way you can get all new things and customize it the way you like it. And you can't beat the price."

"What are they asking?"

"Nothing. It's free. It's been vacant for a while, but it's in good shape. It would be an improvement."

"Easy for you to say." The dragon, for the first time, sounded unsure of himself. "Why should I leave this place? Think of all the packing I'd have to do. Moving is such a pain. I don't even have any boxes."

"You have all those treasure chests," Marco said.

"You can move a few of them at a time," Ellie added.

Silence. Then Hotshot said, "If I like it—and there's nothing to say I'll like it—when can I move in?"

They stifled their triumphant cheers. Their plan had worked! At least, so far. *One thing at a time*, Marabel reminded herself. She tried to sound casual as she said, "As soon as you agree to let us go and promise not to tell anyone we've left, we'll give you directions."

"That soon?"

"That soon," Marco said.

An agonizing silence, and then they heard the most wonderful sound in the world—the scrape of the bolt being pulled back.

Ellie flung herself on the door and tore it open. She fled into the dragon's chamber and from there into the corridor. Marabel ran after her and barely managed to grab her arm

208

before she reached the stairs. "Only a few more minutes, and we'll be out of here," she promised. "Try to stay calm. If they hear you, they'll toss us back in the dungeon for sure."

The threat was enough to quiet Ellie, but her eyes were wild. Marabel could tell she wouldn't be able to stay cooped up any longer.

Floriano had finished giving Hotshot directions to the cave, and the dragon began emptying out treasure chests and filling them with his possessions. Before Hotshot shut the lid, Marabel caught a glimpse of a pair of nail clippers as long as her wooden sword; a bottle marked SCALE POLISH, LEMON SCENT; several fire extinguishers; some enormous, comfy-looking bedroom slippers with holes cut out at the ends for his claws; and a painting of a red dragon with the word *Mother* written on the frame in fancy script.

"Run along now," he said over his shoulder as he opened a second chest. "Good luck and all that. Drop by the cave anytime."

Ellie tugged on Marabel's arm. "Let's *go*," she said between her teeth.

Marabel cracked the door and looked both ways. Seeing no one, she motioned at the others to follow her, and they eased out into the corridor and headed for the stairs.

The basement was deserted, except for the occasional bug. The air was thick with damp.

Marabel saw one of the red WAY OUT signs and hurried toward it, going past the gift shop they'd seen advertised. It was closed.

A sign directed them to a side door leading out of the castle. They looked at one another, swallowed nervously, and pushed it open. Late-afternoon sunlight poured in on them.

A few people were around—gardeners, servants polishing the windows, and a bored-looking sentry—but nobody was looking for them ... yet. "Act casual," Marabel said under her breath, although her heart was pounding hard. She wanted to break into a run but forced herself to stroll casually toward the road.

"Just a few more steps!" Marabel said to encourage her companions. Then, just as they were on the brink of freedom, a trumpet sounded behind them, and a deep voice called from high up in a castle tower, "The prisoners! They're escaping! To arms, to arms!"

Marabel, Marco, Ellie, and Floriano exchanged horrified glances and fled across the green lawn toward the forest. "Hurry! Hurry!" cried Floriano. He could have easily outpaced the soldiers, but he hung back.

Marabel cried, "Run, Floriano! Run home and get help!" But the unicorn shouted, "I'm not leaving you humans to face them alone!"

Another trumpet blast sounded. Feet pounded on the road, making the air rumble like thunder.

And then they were surrounded. Floriano lowered his head and shook his horn at the soldiers.

A familiar-looking goblin stepped out of the crowd. Marabel narrowed her eyes and exclaimed, "You're the one who threw me into the dungeon!"

He bowed. "General Bob Goblin at your service, ma'am."

She ignored the mockery in his overly polite tone. "By what right do you stop us?" she demanded.

"Just following orders, ma'am." He sounded amused. "Her Majesty said not to let you out until she gave the command. I've heard no such command, so it's back to the dungeon with you, and this time we'll make sure you don't make a break for it."

"And what if we refuse to go back?"

"We'll have to drag you, then."

"You're awfully brave!" Ellie broke in. "There must be—what? Twenty of you? All with swords and shields and things. And there are just four of us, and we don't have any weapons, not unless you count Floriano's horn. You wouldn't be so brave if Marabel's father was here with his soldiers!"

"Soldiers of Magikos," the goblin general scoffed. "I don't think we'd have much trouble with them." He broke into a grin. "You *do* have a weapon, though."

"We have nothing," Marco said. "Not even a butter knife."

The general pointed to the wooden sword at Marabel's waist. All the soldiers burst out laughing.

"Tell you what," the general said, still with a sneer that made Marabel clench her fists and her teeth, "you fight me with your sword, and I'll fight you with mine. If you win, you can all go free. If I win, it's back to the dungeon with you."

"Don't be ridiculous," Floriano said to the goblin. "Marabel has only a wooden practice sword, and yours is made of metal!"

"It's all right, Floriano," Marabel said. "Better to die trying than to go back and be turned into a frog."

Marco turned to the goblin general. "We ac—"

"Wait!" Marabel said, remembering the bridge troll. "Just wait. We have to define terms."

"No terms," the goblin said. "Standard rules. Take it or leave it." He unsheathed his sword, a heavy-looking, businesslike weapon with a large grip.

Marabel pulled the battered wooden sword out of her belt and extended it, hilt-first, to her brother. He shook his head and put his hands behind his back.

"But, Marco—" She stopped, bewildered. What was he doing?

"You do it, Mara. You have to fight with him. You're a much better fencer than I am."

"No, I'm not! Lucius always said *you* were better than *me*."

"Lucius always said *you* were better than *me*."

A little laugh escaped her, even through her terror. "He must have told both of us the same thing to make us practice harder!"

Marco laughed, too, and for a moment they felt as though they were back at home, sharing a joke that no one else understood.

Then Marabel got serious again. "But, Marco, you're the Chosen One! The Book says, 'When the Chosen One recognizes himself, he shall prevail.' Doesn't that mean that you're supposed to do the fighting?"

Marco said, "What does that mean about recognizing yourself? I don't think I've done any recognizing."

"Quit stalling!" called the goblin. "What, too afraid to fight?"

Marabel ignored him. She turned the sword around

and held it by the hilt again, thinking of all those hours she had spent in the tower room, with Lucius teaching her the proper grip, the correct stance, the attack and the defense, the rules of chivalric combat, the basics of strategy.

She would hate for her adventure to end here in defeat, after all they had gone through. She remembered how she and Ellie had braved the tunnel, how she had fought off the man-wolf, outwitted the bridge troll, and escaped from the giants. She remembered how she had figured out that the false Floriano was a faery trying to lure them into the faery realm, and how her plan had convinced Hotshot to release them. Her heart glowed with pride, and her right arm warmed and tingled.

She realized that everyone had stopped talking. They were all staring at her, not only Marco, Ellie, and Floriano, but the goblin soldiers as well, some with mouths hanging open. She looked around. "What?" she asked, confused.

"Marabel." Marco's voice was hoarse. He cleared his throat. "Marabel—look at the sword."

The general's sword? No, she followed her brother's gaze to the wooden sword in her hand.

Only, it wasn't a wooden sword.

It was gleaming steel, and it shone like a flame. Had something enchanted it?

She had no time to wonder. She didn't know how, but she could tell that the new sense of pride and confidence that glowed in her heart had flowed into the gleaming blade.

Marabel turned to face the goblin general and took a fighter's stance. It was her turn to sneer. "Still want to fight me, *Bobby*?"

For his answer, the goblin general lifted his own sword.

They circled, each looking for a weakness. Marabel noted that one of the goblin's knees was stiff, and calculated how that would hamper him. She noted out of the corner of her eye where gaps appeared in his leather armor as he moved. She remembered that the goblins wore no shoes. If she could do something to make him stub his bare toe, that might throw him off.

"Ha!" the general thrust his sword at her. She easily hopped out of the way, being careful to go in the direction of his stiff knee so he'd be slow to follow her. She gave an experimental thrust back to gauge the speed of his reaction.

Marabel realized, to her deep astonishment, that despite their desperate situation, she was enjoying herself. This was what Lucius had trained her for—never knowing that he was preparing her to fight a goblin soldier one day, all the way in the Desolate Barrens, but preparing her just the same.

This was what she was meant to do.

Marabel let herself fall into range of the goblin's sword, and then twirled out of his reach again. He was breathing hard. He must be hot in the evening sun, wearing all that leather. Meanwhile, she had just been eating and playing *Impcraft* all afternoon, and her new outfit was light and cool. If she could wear him out . . .

And then she made a mistake. She let him get too close, and his sword sliced her upper arm.

"Marabel, stop!" Marco cried. "Surrender!"

She ignored him. The cut wasn't deep enough that she'd lose a dangerous amount of blood. It hurt less than many injuries Lucius had inflicted on her, but it *was* enough to make her mad. She lunged at the goblin, and he swung his shield in front of his body, just as she'd known he would— just as Lucius had done in the tower on her birthday. She dodged to her opponent's other side and slammed the flat of her sword against the backs of his knees.

Exactly like Lucius on that day that seemed so long ago, Bob Goblin's feet flew up, and he thudded onto his back. Before he could even try to rise, she had leaped on him. She straddled him and held the point of her sword to his throat.

The goblin soldiers murmured and moved closer.

"Back!" she cried. "Back, or else I'll . . ." She didn't know what she was going to say after that and was relieved when they retreated a step.

"Are you a goblin of your word?" she asked the general. He nodded slightly, his wide-open eyes fixed on the bright blade. "You said that if I won, we would all go free. Did you mean that?"

"I did," he croaked. "You can all go. We won't try to stop you."

"By rights, I could kill you," she said. She poked his neck a little harder with the tip of the sword—not enough to pierce the skin, but enough to scare him.

He closed his eyes as though preparing for death.

Marabel savored her victory a moment longer. Then she stood and slid her sword back into her belt, watching with surprise as it turned back to battered wood.

Marco came and put his arm around her shoulder, and only then did she realize that she was shaking.

Two goblins helped their general to his feet. He, too, was shaking. One of his men handed him his sword. He knelt and extended it hilt-first to Marabel, the traditional act of the vanquished to the victor. She took it and held it uncertainly. Lucius had never taught her what to do with a conquered enemy's weapon.

The goblin said solemnly, "Since you spared my life, I will also give you a gift."

From the pouch at his waist, the goblin pulled out a bracelet. It was black and very plain. It wasn't made of silver or gold, and it bore no gems. An odd sort of gift for sparing his life, Marabel thought.

Marabel held out her wrist and the goblin strapped it on. "If you are ever in need of help, Princess Marabel, you may use this to call me, and wherever I am, I'll come."

"Oh!" Ellie said. "I've heard of these things. You turn them around three times or hold them under the full moon or something, right?"

"Nothing that complicated. Watch." He cleared his throat. "Hey, Scari," he said into a similar bracelet on his own arm.

"Hey yourself," came a woman's voice.

"Call Marabel."

The bracelet on Marabel's wrist chimed and vibrated, and she jumped. "What was *that*?"

"That was Scari," he said. "She's an imp—or rather, she's one of the imps—who lives in your bracelet. They're all named Scari. Go ahead, answer her."

Cautiously, Marabel raised the bracelet to her wrist and said into it, "Hello?"

The same woman's voice answered her. "Call from Bob G."

"What am I supposed to do?" Marabel asked, and Bob Goblin showed her how to answer the call and then how to make one herself. Then he beckoned over one of his medics, who bandaged the cut on her arm.

The general saluted her. "Remember," he said, "if you find yourself in danger, call me and I'll come as fast as I can."

"Thank you," Marabel said. "Oh, and, General?"

"Yes?"

"One more thing. Could you make sure that none of the other soldiers follow us until we're well away?"

"Other soldiers?" he asked. "Miss, there *are* no other soldiers on duty at the castle. The rest are all preparing to leave for Magikos."

"What?" Marabel cried. "They're leaving? All of them? When? Why?"

"As soon as they can," the general answered. "We're under threat. A messenger arrived and told us that the Magikian king was going to attack us if Her Majesty didn't return the prince. You three should stay here until it's all over. It looks like it will be dangerous."

The goblin general saluted again, and then he and his soldiers marched across the lawn and into the castle.

Marabel felt numb as she watched them go. So her father's messenger had arrived while they were in the dungeon. No wonder they hadn't encountered any guards during their escape, and the regular afternoon check on the dungeon hadn't been made. No soldiers were left to guard the castle, much less look in on the prisoners.

Yes, they were free. Yes, Marco was out of the dungeon. But they were in enemy territory far, far from home, and Magikos was in danger. Mab was preparing to attack Magikos with her army of Evils, and Marabel and her companions wouldn't be able to stop her.

They had no food, they were exhausted from their long journey, and worst of all, the road home was fraught with danger.

The others looked at her expectantly.

She wouldn't fail. She *couldn't* fail. She would try to get home and help. If something went wrong, at least she'd know she'd done her best.

Marabel handed Marco the goblin's sword, and he slid it into his belt. "Let's get going," she said.

Then high above them came a loud *whirr*, and something blotted out the sun. Ellie cried out, Floriano gave a shrill whinny, and Marco looked around wildly. Before Marabel could move, much less call Bob Goblin on her bracelet, whatever was flying overhead landed with a *whomp* behind her.

"Book protect us," she whispered. "Book protect us, because I'm not sure *I* can."

17

old up there, folks!" It was Hotshot, and he sounded angry. They cowered as the dragon flared a huge flame over their heads. "That was a great landing," he said. "I'm an expert in landing, if you'll notice."

"Expert!" Floriano muttered. "He nearly flattened us."

The dragon turned to the unicorn. "You!" he snarled. "Big problem here. Frankly, you lied to me."

"What?" Floriano nearly choked with indignation. "What are you talking about?"

"You deliberately sent me the wrong way. There's no

cave where you told me to look for it." He shuffled closer, smoke billowing from his nostrils. They stepped back.

"You've already been to the cave?" Marabel asked. He must fly faster than a bird to have made that round-trip in such a short time.

"I tried," Hotshot said. "The first part was easy for someone like me, with those incompetent guards. They should be fired, all of them."

"You didn't eat them, did you?" Marco asked.

"Or burn them up?" Ellie sounded horrified.

"No," said Hotshot. "Would have attracted too much attention. I carried them back and popped them into your dungeon. No one will find them for a while—I left a 'Do Not Disturb' sign on the door. Believe me, the guards will pay attention to it!" That might slow down the guards, Marabel thought, but her aunt Mab wouldn't pay any attention to such a sign. And the thrennight was almost up!

Hotshot turned to Marco. "But what I want to know is, why did you tell me there was a beautiful vacant cave out there? I followed your directions perfectly, my friends, and it doesn't exist. Crooked humans."

"It does, too!" Ellie said. "We spent the night in it!"

"It's a conspiracy," Hotshot said darkly. "You're all in this together. There's no cave, and there never was any cave.

Nobody there ever even *heard* of a cave, except for one that's so small that even the elves who lived in it were complaining about the rent. I don't see why I shouldn't turn you over to the queen. Better yet, I should crisp you up right here." He let a slender flame flicker out of his mouth.

"Wait," Marabel said hastily. "You must have misunderstood Floriano's directions." But maybe the dragon was right. Maybe the cave really was gone. For all she knew, in the Barrens, even big things like caves disappeared. She was getting tired of magic. It was too unpredictable.

Hotshot said indignantly, "I'm an excellent listener. There's nothing wrong with my hearing. Everyone knows that unicorns are liars. What you have here, folks, is a crooked unicorn."

"He's not crooked," Ellie said indignantly. "Maybe he made a mistake. It isn't like we were taking notes when we came here about which direction we went and when we turned, and things like that. You can't blame Floriano!"

"I can blame whoever I like," the dragon said. "When it comes to blame, my friends—"

Marabel interrupted him. "We can't stay out in the open like this," she said. "Anyone looking out a castle window can see us. Listen, Hotshot, Floriano had no reason to lie to you. Why don't we show you in person where the cave is?"

"Show me?" the dragon sounded dubious. "I'm supposed to trot along after you, carrying these heavy bags, while you make your slow human way through the forest? Not Hotshot. I have better ways to spend my time."

"Of course you do," said Marabel. "You're a very important dragon. So why don't you carry us?"

"Just what I was about to suggest," Hotshot said. This was obviously untrue, but it was fine with Marabel if he took credit for her idea, as long as they got away as quickly as possible.

"We humans can get on your back, and you can carry Floriano with your feet," Marco said.

"I know, I know," Hotshot said irritably. He lay down flat and stretched his wings to both sides. It was amazing how big he was. "Board by row number, please," he said.

Ellie climbed onto the dragon's neck. Marabel took her place right behind Hotshot's wings, and Marco sat behind her. Marabel gripped the dragon with her knees. Fortunately, despite its shine, Hotshot's skin wasn't slippery, and the scales gave his passengers something to grip.

Floriano squealed as the dragon tightened a clawed foot around him. "I can't breathe!" he cried.

"If you can talk, you can breathe, believe me," the dragon said. "Would you rather I dropped you? I'd be glad to do that. Just say the word."

Hotshot launched into a speech. "Welcome aboard DragonFlight 1313, nonstop to Cave. This is Captain Hotshot speaking. In the unlikely event that we need to gain altitude, the air will get thin. That means you'll faint, and you'll probably fall off. No refunds. In the event of a water landing, swim. Don't bother trying to fasten your seat belt because there aren't any. No smoking on board except by the captain." He puffed smoke out his nose and chuckled. "A little joke," he said, and then went on. "Due to the shortness of our flight and the lack of flight attendants, there will be no cabin service, so I hope you're not hungry. Now sit back, relax, and enjoy the flight, okay?"

The dragon extended his long, batlike wings and rose with a lurch that nearly threw off his passengers. The jolt made Marabel bite her tongue. She dug her knees into the dragon's sides even harder and clutched the nearest scale.

They rose rapidly above the tops of even the tallest trees. Marabel kept her eyes squeezed shut when they tilted into a turn, as the dragon responded to Floriano's shouted directions. After a few minutes she cracked her eyelids and peered down. She gasped and tightened her grip. Everything was so far away, and Mab's castle was rapidly shrinking behind her.

On their way to the castle, she had concentrated so

hard on surviving and on reaching Marco in time that she hadn't really noticed her surroundings. Now she saw that despite the horror stories everyone in Magikos told about the Desolate Barrens, the realm was beautiful. The bright moonlight showed majestic trees lining the roads, and small villages that looked bustling and prosperous. They passed over a line of dwarves on their way home from work, singing as they approached a cozy-looking cottage. A group of ogre children played in a meadow, their long, skinny arms and legs making them look like spiders. Tiny lights danced in a field; at first she thought they were fireflies, but then she realized that they were moving in complicated patterns to a very definite rhythm. *A fairy dance?* she wondered, but they passed over the lights before she could see more.

A few minutes later, they crossed a wide, deep crack in the ground. As Marabel realized that it was the chasm around the giants' mountain, the mountain itself rose in front of them and Hotshot banked steeply to the right. As they curved around the peak, Marabel caught sight of one of the giant children standing in the doorway of their towering house, looking up at them, her mouth hanging open. She squawked, "Mama!" And then they crossed the chasm and left the giants far behind them.

It had taken days to get from the giants' home to Mab's

castle on foot, and now they had retraced that path in mere minutes. Flying really was the only way to go, she decided.

They were close to home now! What a welcome Marco would receive! Their father would be so proud of Marabel for rescuing him, and for the way she had outwitted and outfought all the dangers they'd encountered. When she showed him the gleaming metal sword, he'd understand that there was something special about her, something that turned wood to steel and gave her courage and skill. She couldn't wait to see little Malcolm, Maisie, and Maria, and of course Lucius.

"Turn left here," Floriano called up to Hotshot.

"Left? You told me to turn right after the giants' mountain! No wonder I couldn't find it!"

"No, I didn't! I said—"

Marabel stopped listening. She turned and looked over her shoulder at Marco, who was grinning with delight as he gazed down at the landscape far below them.

"Isn't this amazing?" she asked.

"Best thing ever," he agreed.

It was dark now, except for the light of the stars and the full moon, and the only way she could tell they were passing over a village was by spotting a group of houses with candlelight shining through the windows. Was this Cornelius's village, or a different one? Which one was Cornelius's home? Marabel wished she could tell him and his mother how successful their quest had been.

Marabel leaned forward and tapped Ellie on the shoulder. She pointed at a bridge where someone was reading a book by torchlight. The reader was sitting under what looked like the troll gate. Ellie looked back at her with a smile.

Now the dragon called back to his passengers, "Prepare for landing!"

"Prepare how?" Marco shouted.

"Hold on tight!" Hotshot yelled. He flew lower and lower until they were barely above the ground, which whizzed by at a terrifying speed. From below, Floriano gave a panicked whinny. The dragon bent his wings to slow them down but they were still going awfully fast when he dropped Floriano. And then, with another *whomp*, he landed.

Ellie slid off the dragon's neck, followed closely by Marabel and Marco.

Floriano appeared from the other side of the meadow, limping slightly. Marabel expected him to complain, but instead, he held his head high and pranced as well as he could. "What an adventure!" he said. "Wait till I tell that stupid donkey. Now I see why my cousins the hippogriffs talk about flying all the time!"

"What's a hippogriff?" Ellie asked Marabel.

"A horse with wings," she answered. "I think most of them live in the same land as those centaurs."

"So where's this cave?" Hotshot broke in. "I'm starting to think you made it up so I'd let you out of the dungeon."

"No, it's close," Marabel said. "It's just over . . ." She broke off and looked around. Where *was* the cave? "If only we had some light!"

"Stand back," the dragon said. They leaped away as he pursed his lips, and like someone spitting out a melon seed, he popped a little flame from his mouth. It landed on the tip of a pine branch, which burst into flames. Marco managed to break the branch off the tree without getting burned, and with this blazing torch to light the path, they made their way to the cave entrance.

"I hope he likes it," Ellie whispered to Marabel.

"Me too! If he doesn't, he might take us back to Mab's castle."

"Or burn us up right here."

That was something that hadn't occurred to Marabel, and she hurried to catch up with the dragon.

"As you can see," she told him, "this is an up-and-coming neighborhood. There's a road nearby that's convenient to shopping, and you have running water right outside your door."

"I've got to be honest, it sounds like it'll be damp," the dragon said.

"Oh no! It's dry as can be. You'll see." She crossed her fingers for luck.

"Here we are," Floriano called. Marabel held her breath, hoping that the dragon would fit, and after he ducked his head and squeezed his shoulders together, he did.

After an agonizingly long minute, the girls heard, "This is huge. HUGE!" They exhaled deep sighs of relief as the dragon went on, "Here's the perfect spot for my piano! And my treasure will fit nicely in this side cave. If I put my table over here . . ."

The girls high-fived. *Success!*

Marco grinned. "Phew! I didn't know that riding a dragon would be such hard work."

Marabel realized that she ached all over, especially her legs and her back. "We have to keep going," she said. "Mab's army's been gone a long time and may already be there. Mab will probably get there soon herself. I want to arrive before she does."

"We can't leave tonight," Ellie said. "We're all exhausted. I don't want to go stumbling over rocks and roots in the dark, and it will be hard to find the opening of the tunnel at night. We have to wait until daylight."

"We have a torch," Marabel reminded her.

"That would make us visible to anyone looking for us," Marco said. "Anyway, that torch won't last all night."

As though it had heard her, the torch flickered and went out.

Marabel had to agree reluctantly that they were right.

They were so tired that the voices of Hotshot and Floriano discussing color palettes and granite countertops versus marble didn't keep them awake. Marabel slept deeply for the first time in days. Tomorrow they'd be home.

Only a few hours later, Marabel sat up with a start. She'd heard a twig snap.

She held still, barely daring even to breathe. Something rustled in the woods. It moved cautiously, but took such long strides she knew it had to be something very tall. A giant?

In the early light of dawn, Marabel found her wooden sword. The rustling continued, one step after another. Then it stopped.

The sky grew even lighter, and now she could make out, between herself and her sleeping companions, what appeared to be a tall stump with long, crooked branches.

The stump moved again, and extended itself a little upward.

With a yell of "Magikos!" Marabel sprang forward and grabbed the thing. She held the edge of her sword against it. "Don't move or I'll cut off your . . ." Was that its head?

The others leaped to their feet, and a puff of flame came out of the cave. Ellie's eyes widened.

"Cornelius!" Marabel cried.

18

So that truly *was* a dragon flying over the village!" Cornelius said. "A splendid sight, but alas, none would believe me when I reported it. I'm pleased that I'll be able to tell them back home that I spoke truthfully. Dragons are rare indeed near our village, especially lately. Most villagers are glad of this scarcity, since the fire breathers cause mischief wherever they roam. But I have always yearned to see one."

"Don't tell them quite yet, will you?" Marabel asked anxiously. She dropped kindling on the glowing coals she had found in the cave.

"Never fear, my lady," Cornelius said. "If I were to speak on this with my compatriots, I would tell them that Sir Hotshot is a dragon of rare wit and benevolence and must be spared their wrath."

"Thank you," Marco said. "He's not really that bad, once you get to know him."

Marabel smiled to herself. That was so Marco! He'd been kept imprisoned by a fire-breathing reptile for almost a thrennight, and he still managed not to hate Hotshot.

Marco started to add a big log to the fire, but Marabel stopped him. "It's too soon—you'll put it out," she said.

"You've learned a lot of things on this trip!" Marco said. "I wonder what Maggie will think when she sees you working!"

"Were you looking for us when Marabel found you?" Ellie asked Cornelius. "Or were you just trying to get a closer look at Hotshot?"

"At first, that was my motivation," he admitted. "I desired to examine the creature from closer up, and if possible, to converse with him. A dragon must have much wisdom to impart!"

Marabel knew that if she looked at Marco, she'd burst out laughing at the thought of Hotshot saying anything wise, so she kept her eyes fixed on Cornelius.

"What do you mean, 'at first'?" she asked.

"As I was making ready to depart my village on a voyage of discovery," the ogre said, "a visitor arrived with a warning."

"What kind of visitor?" Marco asked.

"A faery. One well known to us as a mischief-maker, who likes to lure unsuspecting people and beasts into his realm."

"Wait a second!" Marabel broke in. "Is he tall? Does he have a pointy beard and a curly mustache?"

"Does he wear blue-and-purple robes?" asked Ellie.

"Does he have a—what do you call that thing?" Floriano turned to Marabel. "You know, that thing made of glass?"

"A mirror."

"A mirror, right," Floriano said. "And can he change into a beautiful unicorn when he wants to?"

Cornelius, looking bewildered at the barrage of questions, answered, "He is much as you describe, and is, in addition, a fair shape-shifter. As for mirrors, I know not whether he possesses one. Like all faeries, he owes no allegiance to the queen or anyone else. His sole motive in telling us about your escape is the delight he would find in causing you grief. In addition, he seems to hold some grudge against our friend Sir Floriano." He bowed in the unicorn's direction.

"It's got to be the same guy," Marabel said. "So what did he want, Cornelius?"

"He told us that word was trending on Flitter that some prisoners of the queen had escaped, and that furthermore, the queen's great dragon had vanished at the same time. He asked if any of us had seen these fugitives."

"You didn't tell him anything, did you?" Marabel asked anxiously.

"Never fear, my lady! When you came to our village, you were going *toward* the castle, not away from it, the way escaped prisoners would do, so none suspected that you might be the ones the queen was seeking. And since none else in the village believed that in truth a dragon had over-flown us, none told the faery that such a beast had been near."

"Phew," Marco said.

"But I knew that what I had seen was in truth a dragon," Cornelius continued, "and since the prisoners were said to include two young maidens and a blue-and-gold unicorn in their number, I was most hopeful that it was indeed you and that I would find you."

"I'm so glad you did," Marabel said.

Cornelius looked sheepish before he went on. "Now that I have confirmed that it is this fair company that attends the great beast, I would ask a boon."

A boon, Marabel knew, was a favor. "What kind of boon?" she asked.

"As you well know," he said, "I've been longing to see your land. I heard you tell my mother that you had found an opening in the Wall. I would ask that you take me with you to that door so that I, too, may see what lies beyond it."

"Are you sure?" Marabel asked. "Magikos is different from the Barrens. There aren't any ogres there, except in—" She stopped herself before saying, "except in zoos," and went on, "and people might be afraid of you." He looked so hurt that she added quickly, "Oh, *we* know you're not dangerous. It's just other people."

"If he's with us, it should be fine," Marco said. Marabel wasn't sure, but Cornelius looked so eager that she relented and agreed.

So after a quick farewell and thanks to Hotshot, who barely looked up from ordering and reordering his treasure, they took to the road.

"Did I really frighten you back there?" Marabel said as they made their way through the trees.

"Nigh unto death," Cornelius said solemnly.

Despite everything that was going on, Marabel chuckled to herself. Served him right, after the way *he* had terrified *her* at their first meeting!

They traveled as fast as they could manage. Marabel asked the ogre to keep an eye out for a gigantic door standing by itself among the trees. Cornelius scouted the territory but none of them were sure exactly where it was. Marco had been only semiconscious when Mab and Veneficus had taken him through the door, and Marabel and Ellie and Floriano had been lost when they'd stumbled on it before. She was afraid they'd have to search for it for a long time, and the thought of Mab's army approaching made her frantic with worry.

But they didn't have to search long. They heard a bang and then an ogreish howl from up ahead. Cornelius returned, rubbing a lump on his forehead. "There came a wall where no wall was before!" he said ruefully.

"That's it!" Floriano said. "Lead us to it!"

"I only hope you can unlock it from this side," Ellie said.

But when they found the door, to their surprise and relief, it gaped wide open. "Didn't you close it behind us after we came through?" Marabel asked Ellie.

"I thought *you* did," she answered.

"Who cares?" Marco broke in. "It's open—let's go!"

When they finally neared the palace, Marabel sent Cornelius and Floriano ahead. The ogre looked grave when they returned. "The royal troops surround the palace and are keeping a lookout," he said.

Marabel didn't want to be seized by her father's soldiers

and be dragged into the palace like a naughty runaway child. That would hardly be a fitting end to her great adventure! She wanted to appear before him in triumph, with Marco.

"We know another way in," she told Cornelius. "Follow me."

They passed the tree where they had met the man-wolf. Marabel's pack lay on the trail, ripped savagely open. Ellie turned pale at the sight, and Marabel knew that she was imagining what the Evil would have done to them if he'd caught them. She took Ellie's hand.

The last stretch of open land before they got to the tunnel opening was torture, but they managed to make it across unseen.

Marabel worried that Cornelius wouldn't fit, but he was surprisingly flexible, and he didn't seem to mind walking through the tunnel in a squatting position. "I'm accustomed to it," he said cheerily. "When one finds oneself the lone ogre in a village of humans, one learns to adapt."

They had a moment of anxiety when they found the opening boarded up, but Cornelius shattered the boards with a few blows of his huge fists, and then he helped them clamber out. Marabel was afraid that someone would hear them, but fortunately, they emerged unobserved.

Almost unobserved, that is. As they passed the ancient gray donkey in the corner stall, he commenced braying and kicking the walls. He made such a ruckus that they were afraid someone would come to investigate. Floriano let himself into the stall and the two spoke in hushed whinnies and nickers. They left him with his friend in the stable.

"I guess it's nice to have someone be glad to see you," Floriano said as he waved them good-bye. If that was how the "stupid donkey" welcomed Floriano, Marabel couldn't wait to see the welcome that she and Marco would receive!

The palace was almost empty. Most of the guards, it appeared, were outside, patrolling the grounds and the battlements. At this late hour, Marabel's little brothers and sisters would be in bed, so Ellie slipped off to find her mother, and Marco and Marabel made their way to the royal council room.

Marco and Marabel saw their parents sitting on their thrones, wearing their slippers and bathrobes. The most important courtiers and all the priests and priestesses were also there, talking and arguing furiously. King Matthew looked bewildered. The twins stood uncertainly in the doorway, leaving Cornelius to wait discreetly in the hallway.

The queen glanced up. Her annoyed expression at the interruption instantly changed to uncertainty, then wonder, and then joy, and she screamed.

Guards came running but fell back in surprise when they saw Marco. The king and queen leaped up and hugged him, asking dozens of questions. Marabel tried to speak, but they shushed her and turned to Marco with more questions. Then more guards appeared, dragging an unresisting Cornelius with them.

"Don't hurt him!" Marabel cried. "He's our friend!"

"Your friend?" The king's eyes popped. "What nonsense! Why, can't you see he's an Evil?"

"He really *is* our friend, Father," Marco said earnestly. "I couldn't have gotten home without him." That was perhaps an exaggeration, but it did the trick. Anyone who helped bring the Chosen One home had to be honored, or at least not harmed. The king ordered the guards to release Cornelius but to stand by "in case he goes wild," the king said. "Perhaps if we put him in a cage?"

Marco and Marabel objected so strongly to this that the king agreed that Cornelius could have a guest bedroom, as long as guards stood outside his door.

The guards led him out, and Marabel ran after them. Cornelius shot her a look of misery.

"Don't worry," she said. "We'll get you out of there. I *promise.*"

Marco called her, and she had to go back to where their

parents were waiting to hear the story of the return of the Chosen One.

Maggie gave each of them a hug. "Thank the Book you survived," she said with a quaver in her voice. "But what on earth are you wearing?"

Marabel looked down at herself. She had forgotten her new clothes. Now she suddenly felt half-naked, being surrounded by people in flowing garbs and hooded tunics. But what did it matter what she was wearing? Wasn't the important thing the fact that she had brought Marco home?

"So tell us what happened on your birthday, dear," Queen Maggie urged before Marabel had time to answer. "Where did that evil woman take you?"

Marco, it turned out, had been vaguely aware of his surroundings but unable to move. After they were far enough away from the palace, their aunt had handed him over to her goblin troops. Two dwarves had trussed him up and tossed him into a wagon, and as soon as they arrived at Mab's castle, he was taken to the dungeon, where Marabel had found him.

"Did they beat you in that dungeon, darling?" a worried Queen Maggie asked. "Starve you? Try to make you give up state secrets?"

"He doesn't know any state secrets," King Matthew pointed out.

"Aunt Mab was very nice," Marco said. "She told the guards to treat me like an honored guest, and they did. She let me order whatever I wanted to eat, there were lots of books to read and other things to do there. It was fine, wasn't it, Marabel?"

"Yes, it was very—" Marabel began.

The king looked at her and blinked. "Are you still here, child?"

Why had he thought she wasn't there anymore? She wasn't invisible; this was how they had always treated her. Before, she had been resigned to nobody listening to her. But now she realized that she didn't want to stand for it.

"How did you make your escape?" Symposia asked Marco. "The Book says that when the Chosen One recognized himself, he would prevail. How did that happen? Did you see yourself in a mirror? Come to some deep understanding of your nature?"

"I didn't prevail," he said. "Marabel rescued me."

Everyone turned to Marabel in surprise. Marabel smiled at Marco. At last they'd ask her how she'd done it! She couldn't wait to tell them.

But instead, the queen said, sniffling, "Isn't that just like our darling Marco? He's worried that his sister isn't getting any attention, so he's trying to give her credit for the rescue!"

Everyone murmured in admiration of the Chosen One's generosity of spirit. Everyone except Marabel. She felt like a balloon that someone had pricked with a pin.

"No, really," Marco protested. "She did!"

Marabel added, "I wasn't the only one. Floriano and Ellie did a lot of things on the way there, and then we all worked together to defeat a huge dragon that guarded the dungeon—"

There were horrified gasps at the mention of the most dreaded of all Evils.

"You were guarded by a *dragon*?" King Matthew asked. "My poor boy! It was bad enough having that nasty one here on your birthday. How awful that you had one outside your door for so long!"

"And what do you mean, the unicorn worked with you?" the queen asked. "My dear child, you really must try to make sense!"

"Floriano can talk," Marabel put in. "He—"

Everyone burst out laughing.

"Maybe the girl should be sent to bed," Symposia told King Matthew.

"No!" Marco said. "She's right. Floriano *can* talk, and Marabel *did* save me. When we were caught by goblin soldiers, she had a swordfight with their leader and she beat him! And he gave her a—"

One of the priestesses burst into a cackling laugh. "A fight? With her *sword*? What sword? The one she wears at her waist?"

"Yes. Marabel, show them." Marco turned to her eagerly.

Marabel pulled out the sword and swung it in the air, expecting the blade to turn to steel and reflect the bright candlelight.

No change. No reflection. The sword stayed the same: an old wooden practice sword.

As the whole room, with the lone exception of Marco, erupted into laughter, Marabel turned and ran. She didn't know where she was going—she just ran.

19

Marabel stood alone at the base of the sentry tower and watched the fireworks without interest. Down in the courtyard, musicians played and people danced while the bright lights exploded above their heads. Everyone was celebrating the return of the Chosen One. Marco stood between the king and queen in the balcony far below her. Every time he waved or even looked at the people, everyone cheered.

A familiar step sounded on the stone pavement. Marabel didn't turn around. Lucius took his place next to her and leaned his elbows on the wall. He stood and watched with her, occasionally grunting when a firework was especially beautiful.

"They don't believe me," she said suddenly. She hadn't meant to speak, but once she started, she couldn't stop. "They don't believe I rescued him. Even when Marco tells them I did, they just say isn't he nice for trying to make me feel good. They think somehow *he* rescued *me*." She shook her head, trying to hold back the tears.

"I suppose you're going to say that it doesn't matter," she went on after swallowing a sob. "You're going to say that as long as *I* know what I did, and Marco knows, it doesn't matter what everyone else thinks. But it does matter. It *does*."

"Of course it matters. Only a fool would say it didn't. We all want the people we love to be proud of us. And we all want to be recognized for who we are," Lucius said. His warm hand on hers made her feel a little less alone.

She nodded, looking down at the crowd.

He continued, "Of course, it *is* true that the most important thing is that *you* know what you did and who you are. But I would never say that it's the only thing."

Marabel finally managed to look at Lucius without crying. Something about him sounded different. He looked different, too. He was the same old Lucius, but somehow more than Lucius.

"What do you mean, the important thing is for me to know who I am? I've always known who I am. I'm Princess Marabel of Magikos, sister of the Chosen One."

"True. But that's not all you are. You're also the leader of a team of rescuers, who found her way through a dense forest and overcame many perils and difficulties to save someone she loved." He chuckled. "I thought you were going to give up many times, starting that first night. You would have slept all day in that cave if it had been up to you. And I thought you'd *never* find the door in the Wall."

"I almost didn't," she admitted. "Even though it was right in front of my—wait, what? How do you know about me oversleeping in the cave? And about finding the door?"

He didn't answer, only looked at her, a small smile barely shaping his lips. Realization hit Marabel like a thunderbolt. Could he really be saying what she thought he was saying?

She was so stunned, she had to sit down. "Wait," she said again. "The voice that woke me up in the cave—was that *you*?"

He chuckled. "I had to work hard that night!" he said. "I had to convince Ellie to go on, too. She was ready to give up and go home, remember? She needed a reminder of what was at stake. So I whispered to her, to remind her of her duty. It didn't take much—she's a patriotic Magikian."

Marabel remembered the morning when Ellie had

suddenly changed her mind and decided to continue the adventure, after all. So that was Lucius, not a dream!

"Were you the fairy who told me to use my eyes when I was looking for the Wall?" Marabel asked. "And the squirrel that showed me the signpost to the troll bridge?"

"That squirrel was just a squirrel. But yes, I was the fairy. I was with you on the whole trip. Even before. I was the one who reminded Ellie about the secret tunnel in the stable. She was so young the day her father showed it to her that I was afraid she'd forgotten, so the night before the banquet I arranged with the dream faeries to have her remember that day while she slept."

"You arranged with the . . . there are *dream faeries*?"

"Indeed," Lucius replied. "I knew that Mab was concerned about the state of the magical creatures in her kingdom, and I was worried that she would attack Magikos during the banquet. She always did love drama, even as a girl."

"What about those times when Ellie kept me going when I wanted to give up?" Marabel asked. "Like when Floriano was lost, and I said we should go home and she talked me out of it? Did you or the dream faeries have something to do with that?"

Lucius chuckled again. "No, I didn't have to prompt her those times. That was all Ellie. She's a fighter, that one!"

Suddenly, Marabel felt awkward in front of one of her dearest and oldest friends. "Are you a wizard, Lucius?"

Still with his eyes fixed on the sky, he said, "Something like that. Names don't matter."

"Why didn't you ever tell me before?" she asked.

"I couldn't tell anyone, Princess," he said. "People would always be bothering me for love potions and charms and other silly things. I had—have—a job to do, and I couldn't waste time with little tricks. Besides, your father isn't exactly comfortable with magic."

Now Marabel had to rearrange all her memories of Lucius. Whenever she hurt herself, the bruise or the cut healed quickly after he touched it. Whenever she was sad, his hand on her shoulder made her feel better. Wizards all had their specialties; it appeared that Lucius specialized in sword fighting and healing. The two skills went well together, given how easy it was to get hurt when fighting.

Oh, and he must be good at shape-shifting, if he could turn his lanky self into that tiny fairy.

"So why didn't you tell me what to do on my quest? Why did you tell me to use my eyes, instead of pointing out the door? You didn't have to tell me it was you helping me, and it would have made the trip a lot easier!"

"Would you have learned how brave and clever you are if

I had *told* you what you needed to do?" He shook his head and patted her hand. "No, you had to figure it out for yourself." He nodded at the sword still hanging in her belt. "And when you did, the ancient magic worked."

"What do you mean?" He was making her nervous. It was unlike Lucius to be this serious for so long.

"That sword has been waiting for you for many years," he said softly. "It needed to be wielded by the right person in order to recognize itself, too. That's why it turned into its true self, a blade of steel forged by dwarves many, many centuries ago, only once you realized how much you had accomplished with your wit and your courage. Marco is a good boy, but he wasn't the right person for the sword. The sword knew that. Neither were your father or his sister, nor their father, nor yet his father."

"Wait a second," Marabel interrupted, her heart racing. "How do you know about the sword and how it acted with my father and his father and his father?"

"And his father and his father, and many more. I know because I gave them the sword to practice with, and it never showed itself to be anything but wood."

"*You* gave the sword to my great-great-whatever-grandfather? How old *are* you, Lucius?"

He looked up at the fireworks, now in their final,

extravagant burst. "I've lost track. I studied with your ancestor King Manfred's wizard, the great Callum, if you want to do the math. Callum was an old man himself then, of course."

Marabel's father always talked about "old Lucius," as though the fencing master had already been ancient when the king was a boy. He must be hundreds of years old. Maybe he was under an enchantment that kept people from realizing how old he was. Maybe not. Her father and stepmother didn't really pay attention to the people who worked for them, or wonder about their lives. This was probably the reason why nobody realized how long Lucius had been around.

Marabel looked down at the battered, scarred wooden sword in her belt and sighed. "I guess your sword is broken. It changed long enough for me to save the true Chosen One, and then both of us went back to being our ordinary selves. And I'm not brave, like you said I am. I was scared most of the time."

"That's what true courage is, Marabel—doing what you have to, even when you're scared."

She shook her head. If she was so special, why was she up here on the roof, alone except for Lucius, while hundreds of people cheered Marco as their next king?

"Magikos needs you," Lucius said. "Something is disrupting both sides of the kingdom—this side and the Barrens side. It's as though magic itself is out of balance. Mab has been aware of it for some years, but your father refuses to see the problem."

"But why does Magikos need *me*? Why not Marco? He's the Chosen One, not me. They can solve the problem themselves. No one would listen to me anyway."

Lucius didn't answer. Instead, he asked, "So if you're not going to fight for your country, what are you going to do now?"

She shrugged. "I don't know. I can't go back to the way I was before—not speaking up for myself and letting everyone tell me what to do. Maybe I'll go live with the faeries. Or I'll become a soldier with the goblins. They liked me, and they respected me." She fingered the bracelet given to her by General Bob Goblin. It reminded her of how she had beaten him in the sword fight. "I think I'd make a good soldier."

"You would," said Lucius, suddenly grim, "but you might not be able to leave here for a while."

"What do you mean?" Marabel asked. His tone made her feel cold.

"You might be needed here." His gaze was fixed on a point past the castle wall.

A trumpet blast ripped through the music and revelry

below them. The band stopped playing, the people stopped dancing and cheering, and everyone looked up at the watchtower. Then, a shout: "To arms! To arms! Mab has arrived, and the Evils are attacking!"

Marabel leaned over the parapet, frantic to see what was happening. Lucius took hold of her arm. She tried to jerk free, but stopped when he said in a voice that she recognized from her fencing lessons, a voice that he used only when something was extremely important, "Princess! You must get to safety!"

They made it down the narrow spiral staircase mere moments before a regiment of archers went thundering past.

"Where are we going?" Marabel asked Lucius as they raced toward her chamber.

"You have to lock yourself in your chamber while I find out what's going on." His tone was grim. "Mab and her wizard must have begun their attack."

A shiver of fear ran up Marabel's spine. "What will they do?" she asked, panting.

Lucius shook his head grimly. "Now that she's lost her hostage, Mab must be desperate and her wizard must be furious. There's no telling what Veneficus will do if she can't rein him in."

Ellie was waiting in the doorway. She pulled Marabel inside. "What's happening?" she asked. Marabel shook her head, unable to answer until she caught her breath.

Lucius strode away, calling back, "Lock the door and don't open it for anyone you don't know!"

Marabel closed the door and turned the key with a trembling hand. Being stuck in her room was a lot more frightening than going out and confronting the problem herself. She handed Ellie the key to help calm her. Ellie twisted it in her fingers. "Do you know what's going on?" she asked in a tight voice.

"My aunt is attacking."

"Oh no!" Ellie wailed.

Marabel paced back and forth. It was the middle of the night and they had walked all day, but she was too anxious to feel tired. She wished she could see what was happening outside the castle; not knowing was torture.

"If only I knew what to do," she muttered.

"Do? What do you mean?" Ellie asked.

"We can't let them invade the kingdom and break into the palace! Why doesn't my father even talk to her? We have to do something!"

"There's nothing we can do," Ellie said. "There's a whole army from the Barrens out there. If the Magikian soldiers can't defeat them and the priests can't make them go away, it's hopeless."

"So are you suggesting we should let them do it? Let Mab break in and take Marco again and probably me, too, this time? Veneficus will be so angry we escaped that he'll turn us into something disgusting."

"But how can you stop them?" Ellie asked.

"We have to find Floriano and Cornelius and get their help. We need to work as a team. It took all three of us to outsmart the trolls, remember? And we found the door in the Wall together! Your suspicions about the man-wolf saved us from him, and without Floriano to unlock all those doors, we'd never have made it through the Wall or out of the giants' house."

"True, we all worked together. But *you* were the leader, Marabel. Without you, we would have quit long before we found Marco. We would never have made it."

Marabel stopped pacing and stood in thought. Was it true? Was she really responsible for the success—up till now, at least—of the rescue? She didn't know how that could be possible. Marco was the Chosen One, after all—not Marabel.

Maybe that didn't matter. Maybe, as she'd hardly dared to begin to think, the Book of Fate really was wrong this time—maybe lots of times. Maybe she had to make her *own* fate!

Her heart burned in her chest, and she reached down and drew the sword out of her belt. New courage ran from her heart to her arm all the way to her fingertips, and the wood turned to flashing steel, blazing with an intensity that nearly blinded her.

"Why is it doing that?" Ellie cried.

"It's telling me that I *am* a good leader!" Marabel exulted. "I may not be the Chosen One foretold by the Book of Fate, but that book doesn't know everything. Unlock the door, Ellie—I'm going to fight for my kingdom and my family!"

"Now wait a minute," Ellie said so firmly that Marabel felt herself deflate a little. "Just wait. You might be a great leader, but you don't have anyone to lead. Your father's soldiers aren't going to follow you. You know they aren't."

Marabel lowered her arm. Ellie was right.

But then she looked at the bracelet the goblin general had given her. If she ever needed his help, it was now.

She took a deep breath and said into the bracelet, "Hey, Scari."

"Hey, Marabel," came the reply. "How're things?"

"Not so good. Can you call Bob Goblin for me?"

"What?" Ellie said. "He's Mab's general! Why would he help you?"

"He swore to come to my aid if I ever needed him," Marabel said. "I'm not going to ask him to betray his leader or fight against his own side or anything like that—I only want to talk to her. Maybe he can help with that."

Scari's mechanical voice said, "Trying Bob G." Marabel waited for an agonizing moment, and then Scari said, "He's not picking up. You got his voice-imp. Want to leave a message?"

"Argh," Marabel said. "All right. I guess."

The general's voice came out of the bracelet. "This is General Goblin. I'm either on another line or besieging a castle. Your call is important to me, so please leave a message and I'll get back to you as soon as I can. *BEEP*."

"I need your help," Marabel said into the bracelet. "We're under attack. Um, call me back when you can. Oh, this is Marabel. In the palace. In Magikos."

She looked at Ellie. "Now what?"

Her bracelet chimed. "Hello?" she said eagerly, hoping it was the general getting back to her, but it was only Scari again.

"Not any of my business," the imp said, "but why don't you talk to him in person?"

"I'm not in the Barrens anymore," Marabel said. "I'm at home, in Magikos."

"Duh," said Scari. "Your locator is on. I know exactly where you are. And I know that Bob Goblin is only two hundred thirty-nine point thirteen pebbles away from you."

Ellie leaned over Marabel's wrist. "In what direction?" she asked Scari.

"Northeast."

Ellie's lips moved slightly as she calculated. She turned slightly and pointed out the window. "Northeast. Marabel, he's right outside the castle wall."

"Let's go!" Marabel exclaimed.

Ellie unlocked the door, and they ran through the corridor, down stairs, and up more stairs. As they sped through the final corridor, they heard Cornelius's voice shouting, "I beg of you, good people, set me free! I can be of assistance! I will parley with the other side for you!"

They skidded to a halt. Marabel called, "Cornelius! Where are you?"

A louder flurry of knocks and bangs answered her. She and Ellie followed the sound, and as they rounded a corner, they came upon two guards standing at a door. "Why, it's little Princess Mar—" one of them started to say, when

Marabel pulled out her sword. Not waiting to see if it was wooden or steel, she brandished it in the air.

"Let him out!" she commanded. They gaped at her without moving.

"Didn't you hear me?" she asked. As though her words had released them from an enchantment, they scrambled to do as she said. They fumbled with the key. As soon as the door was unlocked, it popped open, and Cornelius thundered out. Even Marabel and Ellie drew back at the sight of the furious ogre as he picked up the guards like toys and tossed them into the storeroom where he'd been held. The familiar voice of Marabel's mirror said, "Straighten your garbs and comb your hair! You two look a *mess!*" before Cornelius slammed the door and tossed a heavy suit of armor in front of it to keep the guards safely inside.

He turned to them with a smile, looking once more like the sweet Cornelius they knew. "That's better!" he said, briskly rubbing his hands together. "Whither are you bound?"

"No time to explain!" Marabel said. "Come with us!"

They tore down the hallway, through the kitchen, and then out into the kitchen yard. They burst into the stable, ignoring Floriano's startled "Hey!" as they ran past him.

"No time to explain!" Marabel called again, and sped into

the back room to the tunnel opening. Holding her sword high, she climbed over the rubble of the shattered barricade and plunged into the darkness, followed closely by Cornelius, who said, "Ow!" as he banged his head on the ceiling.

Marabel glanced behind her. No Ellie. She looked up the stairs to see Ellie's motionless silhouette, framed in the opening at the top of the tunnel. "Come on!" Marabel called. The Ellie outline shook her head.

Marabel ran back to the foot of the stairs. "What is it?" she asked impatiently.

"I can't," Ellie croaked. "It was hard enough to go in there when we had a torch. I just can't do it in the dark, with only the sword-light."

Marabel hesitated. She wanted the help of her friends but she couldn't wait—things were about to get worse. Mab's army could break through the palace wall at any moment. "I understand, Ellie," she said. "Find someplace safe to hide. Maybe with Floriano. I'll be as quick as I can." She turned and tore through the tunnel.

She stubbed her toe on something she hoped wasn't one of the skulls, and blundered through the damp, smelly tunnel. At long last she stumbled into the stairway, where Cornelius was waiting for her. With his help, she climbed the steps and hauled herself out.

And found herself looking at the backs of Mab's goblin soldiers. Hundreds of them. The sword-light suddenly dimmed and the goblins didn't notice Marabel or even Cornelius.

The Magikian soldiers on the battlements shouted, "Foul beasts! Monstrous Evils! Return to your filthy land! You'll never vanquish Magikos!"

From Mab's soldiers came the shouted retort: "Our queen can beat up your king!"

Just a few feet away, General Bob Goblin strutted back and forth in front of his troops, giving them a pep talk. He shouted, "What do we want?"

"A United Magikos!" they thundered.

"When do we want—" He caught sight of Marabel and stopped abruptly. His eyes widened. The soldiers turned to see what he was staring at, and she couldn't help shrinking back under the surprised gaze of all those fierce-looking purple faces.

"What are you doing here?" the general asked in astonishment. "Don't you know there's a war on? I thought you were still on the other side of the Wall—we all did! We never saw you on the road. How did you get home so fast through the woods?"

"We got a ride," Marabel answered. "No time to explain.

I need you to help me. Your queen is trying to attack my family and turn me into a frog and—"

"Oh, plague it," the general growled. "I thought you were still on the road. It never crossed my mind you'd get here so fast. I would have found some way to avoid attacking if I'd known you were here. I swore an oath to protect you. What do I do now?"

Marabel didn't know how to answer.

The general groaned. "I need to get this sorted out. I have to obey my queen, and she's ordered me to storm the palace. But I owe you my life, and it would be dishonorable of me to harm you."

Marabel waited while the general scowled in thought, stroking his straggly beard as he gazed at her thoughtfully.

Finally, he said, "It's beyond me. I'm taking you to the queen."

Marabel hung back. "No way. She's going to turn me into a frog."

"I won't let her hurt you," Bob Goblin said. "But she's my queen and my boss, and I have to hear her side of things. She'll think of some way to fix this mess."

"No!" Marabel shouted. "You don't understand—she wants to conquer our kingdom!" She turned to run, but the soldiers refused to let her through. She raised her sword to fight her way out of the crowd, but to her dismay, her "weapon" had turned back into wood.

The goblins laughed. "We're not afraid of a toothpick!" one of them shouted.

"Cornelius!" she cried, but he was being held back by a dozen goblins.

She managed to stick the now-useless sword in her belt before two of the soldiers grabbed her. They dragged her along after Bob Goblin, even though she shrieked and kicked.

Cornelius tried to convince the goblins to let them go. "Truly, she is a friend to magical beings," he said earnestly, but the goblins only laughed again and yanked him along, too. Even in her situation, it gave Marabel a tiny twinge of satisfaction to see that it took a dozen goblins, working as hard as they could, to move Cornelius.

Crowds of what Marabel would have once called "Evils" milled around outside the palace. They parted to let the goblin soldiers through, with General Bob in the lead, and Marabel and Cornelius being hauled behind. Creatures of all sorts stared at her: elves, giants, dragons, faeries and fairies, trolls, witches, wizards, man-wolves, an elegant cat wearing boots and a plumed hat, twelve girls dancing in a circle, a family of bears, lots of gnomes, ogres, manticores, and humans.

At their head, wearing brilliant white armor, was Mab. She rode a blood-red horse, and her helmet was pushed back, showing her gleaming dark hair and proud face. She appeared to be conferring with a giant, who was bent over, his hands on his thighs, in order to hear her better.

When Mab spotted General Bob Goblin leading Marabel, her face showed first surprise, then—to Marabel's confusion—relief, and finally triumphant glee, which turned Marabel's knees to jelly. She would have crumpled to the ground if the goblins hadn't been holding her so tightly.

"How did you get here? And what have you done with my dragon?" Mab demanded. Marabel couldn't speak. The queen turned to her general. "You found her!"

"No, ma'am." He stood next to Marabel. "*She* found *me*. And even if you order me to, I can't harm her. She spared my life when all the rules of combat would have allowed her to kill me."

"But I'm your queen!" Mab cried. "And your commander! You *must* do as I say, or be tossed into the dungeon for the rest of your short, miserable life!"

The goblin soldiers murmured and stepped near their general.

"I think not," Bob Goblin said.

Mab addressed the giant she had been talking with. "Sergeant!" she said. "Seize the general and the human girl!"

The giant straightened, but instead of doing as she said, he put his hands behind his back. He repeated General Bob Goblin's words: "I think not."

Mab looked around wildly. "Will *no one* obey me?"

It appeared that no one would. But then a tall, black-clad figure stepped out of the ranks.

Veneficus.

20

At first, the wizard didn't see Marabel. "What do you require, Your Majesty?" he asked Mab smoothly. They might have been chatting in the throne room instead of besieging a palace.

Mab pointed wordlessly at Marabel.

When Veneficus saw her, his lips parted in a thin-lipped smile. He lifted his hand, his long, skinny fingers pointed directly at Marabel's face. A plume of green light appeared in his palm, and his fingers caressed it, shaping it into a ball, squeezing it until it grew as bright as a torch flame. He breathed some unintelligible words, drew his arm back, and—

Marabel wrapped her fingers around the hilt of her sword. Just as Veneficus hurled the green light toward her, she yanked the weapon out of her belt. "Long live Magikos!" she cried, and swung the sword in a wide arc as the ball of light hurtled at her. The blade—gleaming steel again—struck the light with a *thwack*, and she slammed it away.

The flaming ball flew up, up, and over the palace wall. It struck a window in the highest tower, and even from that distance, those watching below heard a tinkle of broken glass. And then pale green light shot out the windows and dissipated.

Marabel remembered what the wizard had said to Mab the day of the kidnapping, about needing time to recharge his magic. Before her aunt had the chance to pull a magical green light from somewhere, Marabel leaped forward. She grabbed Mab and held the tip of her sword against her back.

"You and I," she said, barely able to speak over the adrenaline that made her heart thump and her hands shake, "are going to talk."

Mab's war tent was as spacious as a farmer's cottage, and was furnished with low couches strewn with gaily colored silk cushions.

Marabel and her aunt glared at each other. Marabel was determined not to lose the staring contest. So was Mab, it appeared.

A sudden noise made them break their gaze. Mab moved to the table and picked up a crystal flagon.

"Bluefruit juice?" she asked. The sweet aroma made Marabel think of Lucius.

"Yes, please," she said, and her aunt poured two glasses.

Mab looked up and saw Marabel watching intently. She stepped back and gestured at the full glasses. "You can choose which one you want," she said. "I wouldn't poison my own niece, you know."

"I'm supposed to believe that?" Marabel retorted. "You threw your own nephew into a dungeon and set a fire-breathing dragon to guard him! You said you'd turn him into a frog! How do I know you wouldn't poison me?"

Mab sighed and sat down. Neither seemed in the mood for bluefruit juice anymore.

"Honestly, I wouldn't harm you. I couldn't even bear to punish you harshly for breaking into the castle—remember?"

They'd never even written those thousand lines, actually.

"And it's not only because you're my niece, although that would be enough," Mab said softly. "In truth, I could never bring myself to harm Marianna's children."

Marabel was startled to hear her mother's name. "You knew her?" she asked.

Mab smiled a sad little smile. "She was my best friend," she said. "I knew her long before she married your father." She looked up at Marabel and her smile lost some of its sorrow. "You remind me of her, you know. She was brave, too, although she was always cautious, like Matthew."

Marabel sat down next to her. "I don't know anything about my mother. My father hardly ever talks about her, and my stepmother never knew her. All I know is that she had dark hair like me—is that why I remind you of her?" She longed to hear that she was like her mother.

Mab cocked her head and examined Marabel. "Oh, you do resemble her somewhat. The more I look at you, the more I see it. But I'm not really talking about how you look. It's how determined you are. And clever. And brave!"

Marabel wanted to learn more, but that would have to wait. "Let's get down to business. First of all, you tried to take over the throne from my father, so he banished you? You really want to be queen that badly?"

"I *would* be a much better ruler than Matthew, but that's

not really it." Mab drummed her fingers on the table. "I don't know how much history you've studied. You do know that Magikos and the Desolate Barrens used to be one country, don't you?"

"Of course. But that was a thousand years ago!" Marabel said.

"True," her aunt acknowledged. "Our ancestor King Malcolm was afraid of magic. I don't know why; maybe he was frightened by a witch when he was a baby. So he built a wall and banished most of the magical beasts to the Barrens on the other side.

"At first it worked pretty well, or so they thought. But things in the Barrens are starting to fall apart. Magical beings are becoming dangerous. Faeries are luring innocent travelers to their realm and not letting them go, even when the thirty-day limit is up. Gnomes have been spotted planting poison ivy on forest trails. Some giants are getting out of hand—"

"Giants?" Marabel interrupted. "Do you mean the giants who live on a mountain surrounded by a chasm?"

"Don't tell me you've met them!" her aunt exclaimed. "How did you manage to escape capture?"

"We didn't," Marabel said. "They caught us, but we got away."

"I must say I'm impressed," Mab said. "It's not easy to escape from giants!"

Marabel tried to look modest, but the praise made her beam.

Mab went on, "We could use some help, and your father's council is very good at regulating magic, after so many centuries of practice. If I were ruling both sides of the Wall, I'd have the means to take care of it myself. And I *should* be in charge! I hope you won't think I'm bragging when I say that I've always been smarter than Matthew, and a better leader. Lucius used to tell me I was a good fencer, and he—"

"Lucius taught you to fence?"

Mab smiled. "I loved it! He always teased that your father could beat me, so once I challenged Matthew to a duel. I used only an old wooden practice sword and Matthew used a steel one—blunted, but still a real weapon—and by that time he was much bigger and stronger. Still, in five minutes I had him begging for mercy."

Marabel pulled the wooden sword out of her belt. "Is this the sword you used?" she asked.

"Yes!" Mab took it with a delighted look. "I'm surprised it's held up all these years. It looked almost this bad when I was your age." So Lucius hadn't told Mab how old and magical the sword was—or how old and magical *he* was, either.

Marabel might be the only person in the world who knew the truth about them.

"Are you a better fencer than your brother?" Mab asked.

Marabel didn't know how to answer without bragging, so she said uncomfortably, "I guess so."

"And don't you think you'd be a better ruler of Magikos than Marco? He's a very sweet boy, but does he have what it takes to rule?"

This had never occurred to Marabel. Marco had fulfilled the prophecy in the Book of Fate by being born at the right time on the right day of the right month, and this meant that he was the Chosen One. Even if something happened to keep Marco from becoming king one day, Marabel knew she would never be allowed to sit on the throne. Magikos had never been ruled by a queen, only a king. If Marco couldn't fulfill his duty, the council would find some boy cousin to rule until Malcolm was old enough to take power.

But if Marabel *could* rule, would she want to? Would she do a good job?

The thought was exhilarating. Sitting in that big throne, watching everybody obey her without question, not having to do anything she didn't want to do—who wouldn't want that?

But she knew that being a leader meant a lot more. A good ruler has to have her people's interests at heart, has to be brave and wise and strong, even when she's tired and discouraged. She has to give up things that she wants, if that will make her country stronger and happier. The idea of all that responsibility was daunting.

"I don't know," she confessed. "Marco's the most honest person I've ever met, and he has the kindest heart, and he's so fair that it's sometimes ridiculous."

"Hmph. Those are good qualities, I'll grant you, but they're not everything a ruler needs. A ruler also needs to be strong and courageous, and to be able to think on her feet. She needs to deal with people and beings of all kinds and understand how others' minds work. She needs to be willing to work hard, even when she's exhausted and discouraged. From the little I know of the two of you, you're the one who has those traits—not Marco. It's too bad you weren't the Chosen One! And I'm the one who has those same traits—not Matthew. I should be queen!"

"So if my father doesn't give you the whole kingdom now, you're going to turn me and my brother into frogs?"

"Maybe you'd rather be something else?" Mab asked. "A snake? A scorpion?"

"*What?*" Marabel was shocked at the casual suggestion.

Mab burst out laughing, and then said hastily, "Oh, don't look like that! I'm only joking. All that talk about turning Marco into a frog or a snake—that's all it was, just talk. I was desperate. Ever since Matthew exiled me, I've been writing to him, sending messages, everything I could think of, to get him to let me reason with him. Besides, I won't let Veneficus play around with such dangerous spells, especially with my relatives. Imagine if he was only partially successful!"

They both shuddered. Marabel pictured a being that was half snake, half human, and was glad that her aunt had stopped the wizard from trying out new kinds of magic on them.

And then that imagined half animal, half human gave her an idea.

Marabel and Mab worked out the conditions for the truce. Marabel had a hard time convincing her aunt of some of its provisions, but when they finally agreed on everything, they sent their carefully worded message to the king. They settled in the tent to await an answer.

Mab drummed her fingers on the table. "Matthew is so stubborn," she said, "and he has a hard time admitting when he's wrong." Marabel suspected that her aunt was probably like him in that respect.

Finally, Lucius appeared. "His Majesty requests the presence of both of you in the throne room," the old knight said formally.

"At least he *requests* us to come, instead of ordering it," Marabel said. Mab didn't answer. Could her aunt be nervous?

"Where's Marco?" Marabel asked as they hurried down a corridor.

"In his chamber," Lucius answered. "He tried to stay awake, but both he and Queen Maggie dropped off to sleep and were carried to their beds."

In the throne room, King Matthew was pacing rapidly back and forth on the dais. His ministers, and the priests and priestesses, huddled in a corner, looking worried. He turned to face Mab and Marabel with his hands on his hips, looking so angry that they stopped in their tracks.

"What is this *nonsense* about a truce?" he thundered without saying hello.

"It's not nonsense," Marabel said.

"I'm talking to your aunt, not to you," the king said. "Return to your chamber immediately, young lady. I don't know how you wound up outside the palace, but when I find out, there will be consequences."

The longtime habit of doing what she was told (well,

mostly) almost made Marabel turn and go back upstairs. But she stood her ground.

"It's not nonsense," she said again. "And it's the only hope you have of avoiding a war. Just listen to what we have to say."

"Your daughter is right, Matthew," Mab said. "If you won't at least consider our proposition, my troops will attack. Is that what you want?"

For an instant it appeared that the king did want a fight. But then he flung himself on his throne. "All right," he said. "You have ten minutes."

"First," Marabel said, "change the law so that the ruler of Magikos decides who will be the next ruler. It may be the ruler's oldest child, if that child shows promise of leading well, but it may also be another child, or a trusted adviser, or anyone else who would rule wisely." She looked anxiously at her aunt, who nodded slightly. So far, so good.

"What you want," King Matthew interrupted, "is for me to do away with everything we have always done in Magikos, practices and procedures that have ensured the continuity of the monarchy and the stability of the kingdom for a thousand years. Not to mention ignoring the Book of Fate, the highest authority in the land."

"How stable *is* the kingdom, really, Father?" Marabel broke in. The king looked at her as though surprised that she would question him. "You've been trapped inside the palace for a thrennight, the Wall no longer holds, and your son—and yes, your daughter, although that doesn't seem to concern you much—was held captive and threatened with being turned into something cold-blooded. Does that sound stable?"

The king looked so unutterably sad that Marabel almost regretted her bitter words. "Do you really think your welfare doesn't concern me, Daughter?" he asked.

"It's never seemed to," she muttered.

He sighed and ran his hand over his forehead. "I'm sorry I've given you that impression. It's not that I'm not concerned about you, Marabel. It's that so much depends on Marco. He's the ruler whose birth was foretold by the Book of Fate, and the entire future of our kingdom rests on his shoulders. I've had to pay special attention to him, and I'm sorry if that left you feeling neglected."

"But what if the Book of Fate is *wrong*?" Marabel asked. "There's no Book in the Barrens, and everyone seems to do perfectly fine there. They don't have a piece of paper telling them what's going to happen. They have laws and rules, but they're made by *people*."

"Rules made by people? No Book?" King Matthew appeared to be having a hard time even comprehending the words.

"I understand your difficulty in accepting this, Brother," Mab put in. "I went through the same thing when you exiled me. It was difficult for me to live my life without being able to consult the Book, without it telling me what was going to happen. But now I understand that it's better this way."

"But Marco," King Matthew said. "Marco's birth was foretold, and the Book said he was the Chosen One who would save the kingdom." He quoted, "'The child born at the thirteenth minute of the thirteenth—'"

"Father, couldn't it be a coincidence that he was born then?" Marabel asked. "After hundreds of years of babies being born to the royal family, wasn't it bound to happen sooner or later that one would be born at that time on that date?"

"Maybe the things they wrote down in the Book weren't meant to be laws," Mab said. "Maybe they're just advice, like proverbs. Maybe when it says, 'Never wake a sleeping giant,' it might not mean exactly that, but that you should be careful when you disturb something that could be dangerous."

"Or 'He who comes late to dinner finds nothing but crumbs' isn't a law against letting people eat if they're late," Marabel added. "It might be a way of saying that punctuality is good."

"We're not saying that the Book of Fate needs to be discarded altogether," Mab said. "Just that we might want to look at it as a collection of wise sayings gathered by our ancestors. The sayings can guide us, but I don't think they were ever intended to run our lives."

King Matthew opened his mouth and then shut it without speaking. He looked so confused and worried that Marabel almost didn't have the heart to tell him the final requirement for the war to stop. But she had to.

"One more thing, Father." She took a deep breath. "Magikos and the Barrens need to be reunited. Magical beings need to be able to come here without fearing they'll be trapped in a park or a zoo or a stable."

"Reunited?" he asked feebly.

Marabel nodded. "One country, but with two rulers. You and Aunt Mab." This was the part that they had argued about the longest when they were working out the conditions of the truce. But Mab had finally agreed to stop insisting that the Magikian throne be turned over to her entirely.

"It makes sense, Matthew," Mab said. "I still think I'd be a better ruler than you—"

He made an annoyed sound with his tongue, which she ignored.

"But I'm willing to compromise. Your daughter is very wise, and very persuasive."

The king looked at Marabel as though he wasn't sure

who Mab was referring to. "Marabel?" he asked. "Wise?"

"Yes, Marabel," Mab said. "She thought that the two of us together would make one great ruler, but that either of us alone might not have every necessary quality. Perhaps I was in error when I tried to force you to hand over the throne. I should have suggested co-ruling from the start."

"It wasn't just me," he protested weakly. "The priests— the advisers—all the council members—they all said that it was against the Book of Fate, and that disaster would come if I allowed you to rule. A queen has never ruled Magikos. It would be a crime against the Book!"

"Would it, Brother?" Mab broke in. "I can't recall any part of the Book that says that Magikos must be ruled by a male."

Marabel ran her mind over the passages she'd had to memorize in her Old Magikian class. Huh. When the Book spoke of the Chosen One, it talked about a *child*, not a boy. It never said "king"—it just said "ruler." Old Magikian was a tricky language, but she was sure of this.

This time, Matthew couldn't even answer.

"And, Father," Marabel said, "there's another reason why Magikos should join back together. We're *supposed* to be a magical place. That's our name, isn't it? Magikos?"

"Listen to her," Mab said earnestly. "I think she's figured

out what the problem is. We had a long talk in my tent. Matthew, she reminds me so much of Marianna; she understands people and other beings, and I think she's hit on the cause and the solution to the woes on both sides of the Wall."

At the mention of his late wife, the king's obstinacy melted. "Go on, then, child," he said.

Marabel drew a deep breath. She knew this softer mood wouldn't last long, and if she didn't convince him now, she never would.

"Things are out of balance, Father," she said. "Magical beings are behaving oddly in the Barrens, and nobody knows why. Meanwhile, the wrong kind of magic is happening here. That drought when I was little wasn't a natural disaster. Aunt Mab said that during our drought, the weather was perfectly normal everywhere around us. Something was wrong in Magikos, and only in Magikos."

Her father didn't answer, but he seemed to be listening.

"And the centaurs," Marabel went on. "It's like there's some kind of hole in Magikos where magic should be, only you're keeping out so much magic that the hole won't get filled. Somehow those centaurs that came around felt like something was missing, and they were drawn here. If you allow magic to come back—not just a few good fairies, and unicorns in stables and dragons in parks, but magic the way it was in the days before the Wall—maybe then things will be in balance again."

"Let *Evils* into my kingdom?" The king looked horrified.

"Not all the beings you call Evil really are so," Mab assured him. "There are good faeries and bad faeries, good unicorns and bad unicorns, even good trolls and bad trolls, just like humans."

And good ogres, Marabel thought, thinking of kind, gentle Cornelius.

"In the Barrens, we have laws to keep everyone, magical and non-magical, behaving in a civilized way," Mab said. "General Goblin is willing to confer with your advisers about updating your laws, if you like. You've always been too trusting, Matthew. The little trick that Veneficus played to get us into your palace would never have worked in the Barrens. Our security forces would have seen right away that Veneficus was just pretending to be silly and confused. He knew that your guards would be distracted by the alarm, and that I could take advantage of the diversion to slip in, too."

So that's how they did it, Marabel thought.

The king started to speak, but his sister interrupted him.

"It won't be easy," she warned. "It took a thousand years for things to get so far out of balance between our two lands.

It might take some time for everything to be set right again when we're reunited."

"And maybe…" Marabel started, but she hesitated. She didn't want to go too far, but while he was listening, she wanted to say it. "Maybe we can make our *own* destinies, Father. Maybe there isn't just one Chosen One—we're all the Chosen One in our own lives."

This time, the king didn't even try to answer.

"Let's leave him for a while," Marabel whispered to her aunt. "This isn't the kind of thing you can change your mind about in a minute."

Mab nodded and turned to her brother. "You know where to find me."

The pink light of dawn was beginning to come through the windows when Mab walked Marabel back to her room. Marabel was about to curtsey to her aunt but on an impulse threw her arms around her instead. "Thank you," she whispered. "Thank you for taking me seriously, and especially for making my father listen."

Her aunt patted her back as she returned the hug. "Get some sleep," she said. "I'll come find you in the morning, and over breakfast you can ask me anything you like about your mother. I'd love to tell you about her."

And on that, they parted.

21

The next night, at the auspicious hour of thirteen minutes past thirteen o'clock, Marabel and Marco joined the rest of the royal family on the balcony to the cheers of the people gathered below. Hundreds of flaming torches illuminated the courtyard almost as bright as day.

The crowd was so large that it spilled through the gate, onto the drawbridge, and into the yard beyond. Most of them were Magikians, but the few soldiers from Mab's army who remained in Magikos, both human and magical, were there, too. Humans and magical beings mostly stayed separate, although there was already a little mingling. "Give them time," Lucius had said to Marabel. "Change is hard for some."

In front of King Matthew was an elf-o-prompter loaded with the scroll containing his speech. An elf stood next to it, ready to turn the handle and unroll the scroll.

"My people!" the king began. The elf made a quarter turn. "My sister Mab has returned to Magikos after a long, er, vacation on the other side of the Wall. I am pleased to say that she has agreed to share with me the responsibility of ruling the United Kingdom of Magikos, bringing the Barrens back into the kingdom. We will rule as equals from this day forth. It is our hope that this healing will solve problems on both sides of the Wall. Magical beings in the Barrens have become restless and harmful, while magical beings have appeared on our side, as if there is an imbalance that magic itself is trying to correct."

Murmurs arose from the crowd and the elf finally stopped cranking the elf-o-prompter. He mopped his tiny brow.

"Further," King Matthew went on, "there will be a change in how succession to the throne is handled in Magikos. For the sake of the kingdom—"

"And to keep his big sister from beating him up," Marco whispered to Marabel. She choked back a laugh.

"—we declare that Prince Marco and Princess Marabel will co-rule the United Kingdom of Magikos after us."

The king lifted his eyes from the elf-o-prompter and spoke from his heart. "My dear people, the Book says, '*For, lo! When the Chosen One is recognized, what was broken shall be repaired and harmony shall rule o'er the land. The Chosen One's valor will turn a great threat away from the kingdom and all shall rejoice.*'

"Only now, dear subjects, do I know what those words mean. Perhaps the Book is not as infallible as we have all thought, but I hope we can agree that it's correct when it says that healing is better than remaining enemies. Magikos was broken into two pieces a thousand years ago, and now it must be made whole. What do you say, Magikians? Are you with me in reuniting the broken kingdom?"

Silence from the crowd. Then a chorus of cheers rose from below. "Long live the king and queen!" some shouted, and others cried, "Welcome home, Mab! We've missed you!" Still others shouted, "United Kingdom of Magikos forever!" Marabel made out a few calls of, "You go, Mab girl!"

The king broke out in a smile that showed the same relief that Marabel was feeling in her heart. All the members of the royal family, even little Maria, took turns waving to the crowd. When the people finally stopped cheering and turned to the refreshments and entertainment that had been provided, the royal family went down the stairs together.

"Well!" Queen Maggie said. "I don't think it could have gone any better."

It really was perfect, Marabel thought. Marco was safely home, and she and Ellie and Floriano had had an adventure that people were already writing ballads about. Her father had overcome his pride and stubbornness, and had done the right thing for his country. Lucius, having revealed his true nature to the king, was finally permitted to teach her to fence.

Nothing could go wrong now.

A thrennight later, the long-postponed birthday celebration finally took place. Much less fanfare was planned than for the first attempt. The king and queen had invited only a few guests—"Just some of our closest friends, dear," Queen Maggie had assured Marabel. Marabel and Marco would sit with Floriano, Ellie, and even Cornelius, despite Queen Maggie's worry about how much an ogre would eat. Mab would be an honored guest. (Veneficus had not received an invitation. It was dangerous to slight a wizard in this way, but Queen Maggie refused to allow him anywhere near her family.)

Poppy carried Maria down the steps, and Ellie held Maisie's hand. Malcolm clutched the banister and refused all offers of help. "I'm a big boy!" he proclaimed.

When Marabel entered the banquet hall, she saw, to her dismay, that Ginevra was there, seated next to Marco.

"Are you surprised?" Queen Maggie asked anxiously. "I noticed you talking with her at the birthday party and I thought you would be happy to have her back. Many of the princesses' parents wouldn't let them come, after what happened last time, but Ginevra apparently insisted on being here. She must be a good friend to you!"

Marabel didn't want to hurt her stepmother's feelings, so she said as graciously as she could, "How nice of you to notice. Thank you, Maggie."

The queen smiled with obvious relief. "We decided not to be so grand this time, but to have lots of music and fun activities instead. Your father hired some of those elves— you know, the ones who are so clever at making pictures? And we have—"

A scream interrupted the queen. Everyone looked at Ginevra, who had leaped up and knocked over her chair. Ginevra pointed a trembling finger at the magic detector, where Cornelius stood with his arms stretched wide, while one of the guards ran a wand around him. They were being extra cautious under General Goblin's new regulations.

"What's *that* thing?" Ginevra squawked. "You're not letting it in, are you?"

White-hot anger ran up Marabel's back and she kept her voice calm only with difficulty. "That is our friend Cornelius. He is an honored guest at this party."

"But he looks like an ogre!"

"He *is* an ogre," Marabel said, "and a friend to Magikos. Cornelius!" She waved him over. "I think this is your chair." She pointed at the only seat in the room large enough to accommodate him. "And, Ellie, this is yours, next to mine."

"Many thanks, gracious princess," Cornelius said. He bowed to Ginevra. "I extend my sincere apologies for having affrighted you, my lady."

Ginevra managed to scrape together a little of her usual self-possession. "I wasn't frightened," she said haughtily without looking at him. "I was startled, that's all. I've never seen a—one of them before." She sat back down, and Cornelius settled into his seat, which, Marabel was amused to notice, was straight across from Ginevra's.

"So I hear you had . . ." Ginevra paused as though looking for the right word. She finished, "An adventure."

Marabel nodded.

"Everyone's talking about it," Ginevra said.

Marabel thought, *It must upset Ginevra to hear people talking about something other than her.*

"It doesn't sound like a very princessy thing to do," Ginevra went on.

"It doesn't?" Marabel pretended she was surprised to hear her say that.

"Oh no," Ginevra said. "Adventures mean consorting with all sorts of . . . people." She looked at Ellie, who was taking a sip of bluefruit juice, and then at Cornelius, who had unfolded his napkin and laid it neatly on his lap. "Sleeping out in the open. Using a weapon." She shook her head in disapproval. "Not what *my* family considers appropriate behavior. Of course, things are different in your kingdom." She looked pointedly at Malcolm, who was raising a fuss about something, and Queen Maggie, who was trying to calm him down.

The musicians played a lively tune while servants hurried around with dishes and laid them in front of the diners. Ginevra wrinkled her nose and picked at the food as though it was spoiled, but Marabel ate everything in front of her. It was delicious.

Two elves were at the next table. Explosions of laughter

arose from the guests as the small creatures worked their modest magic to create instant portraits.

"Ooh!" Ginevra exclaimed. "I want to take an elfie with the ogre! Nobody will believe I had dinner with an Evil unless I show them."

Marabel felt an angry response welling up in her, but before she exploded, Floriano trotted up to the table. "Sorry I'm late," he said. "That stupid donkey—"

"Is this the talking unicorn?" Ginevra squealed.

"Floriano, at your service." He bowed gracefully and took his place next to her. Ginevra stared as he ate his salad as tidily as any human. "Ah, that's better," he said. He glanced at Ginevra.

Please don't lay your head on her lap, Marabel begged him silently. Even though that was the usual unicorn behavior, the fussy Ginevra would be sure to object. Luckily, at that moment Ellie asked Floriano a question. The unicorn turned his attention to the other side of the table, where Ellie and Marco were trying to remember something about Hotshot's new cave.

Ginevra reached into her pocket. "Oh, I almost forgot!" She handed Marabel a small package wrapped in red-and-silver silk, her country's royal colors. "Happy birthday from all of us in the Kingdom of Norumbega."

A present? From Ginevra? Maybe Ginevra wasn't so bad. Maybe she wasn't jealous of the attention that Marabel was receiving from across the known world, after all. And maybe she didn't know how to be nice but was trying.

"Please open it now," Ginevra said. "I think it's something you really need. I hope you like it!"

Flushing with pleasure, Marabel untied the string and found a glass bottle that fit in the palm of her hand. A glowing liquid swirled inside it, and fancy letters on the label read BEAUTY POTION.

"What's that for?" Ellie asked.

Ginevra ignored her and addressed Marabel. "Surely you aren't happy with the way you look." Ginevra patted her own glossy black curls as she eyed Marabel's hair, which, up until now, Marabel had thought looked quite nice. Marabel gazed at the bottle, the label hard to read through the tears of hurt and anger swimming in her eyes.

"It doesn't work if someone else puts it on you. You have to do it yourself," Ginevra went on. "It will spread through your whole body and make you beautiful. Or at least pretty. It depends on how much improvement is necessary."

Wordlessly, Marabel handed the bottle back to Ginevra, who looked astonished. "Why, don't you *want* to be pretty?" Ginevra asked.

Before Marabel could think of an answer, Floriano laid his blue head on Ginevra's lap. His horn bumped her wrist, and the small bottle flew out of the princess's open hand. Its top popped off, and the liquid splashed all over her.

"Aieeee!" Ginevra screamed, jumping up from her seat. "You stupid unicorn! You're as big an Evil as that ogre!"

Why was Ginevra so upset? Marabel wondered. Why would she object to a little more accidental beauty?

Then Ginevra's nose widened, and her whole face pushed forward. She stared at her hands as her fingers fused together, and then split into dainty forked hooves.

"What's happening to her?" Marco cried, and Ellie drew back, shock on her face.

"Help!" Ginevra cried as people crowded around her, gasping and murmuring. "Help me! Help meeeee! Eeeeee!" With a final squeal, she dropped down on all fours, and to everyone's astonishment, where the princess of Norumbega once stood, there now was the prettiest pink-and-black pig, a red gown trailing behind her, a crown sliding off her cute little head. She squealed and ran around furiously. She bit ankles and stamped on toes with her sharp hooves. The guests jumped out of her way, which seemed to enrage her even more.

"Whatever happened here?" the king demanded.

Marabel explained rapidly. Her father put his hand over his mouth, but Marabel could tell he was smiling by the way his eyes crinkled.

Mab sniffed the empty bottle. "Oh, I know this potion," she said. "Children in my kingdom use it to play tricks on one another. If she just got a drop or two on her, the spell will wear off in a day."

"It was the whole bottle," Marco said.

"It will take some time, then." Mab's lips twitched. The squealing pig ran after some fleeing guests and skidded on the polished stone floor. "How did it get on her?"

"She . . ." Marabel paused, and then made up her mind. "It was an accident. She was holding it when it spilled, so I guess that counted as putting it on herself. I'm sure she didn't mean to give me a birthday present that would turn me into a pig. She thought it was a beauty potion. The labels must have gotten mixed up."

Her father eyed the pig doubtfully. "Well, she'll have to stay in the barn until she turns back into a princess. I'll tell her parents what happened, and when she's back to her normal self, they can send a swan to take her home."

The pig froze, a look of horror on her face. Lucius picked her up, saluted the king, flashed a grin at Marabel, and left with the wriggling, squealing animal under his arm.

Maggie turned to the musicians. "Play something happy, will you?" she asked, and they struck up a lively tune. Cornelius caught Marabel's hand and pulled her onto the dance floor. Ellie ran to join them, as did Floriano. They showed everyone how to dance in a circle the way they had done at Cornelius's village. Marco and Marabel joined hands and danced and danced.

Lucius was right, she thought as she twirled. *The important thing is what I know in my own heart. And what I know is that I'm capable of great things.* She couldn't wait to find out what they would be.

Her father and Aunt Mab would rule the kingdom together, and, one day, if she and Marco proved their worth, the two of them would sit side by side on matching thrones and be the best king and queen of the United Kingdom of Magikos that they could be.

Yes, everything was perfect now. Her troubles were over. From now on, Princess Marabel of Magikos would live happily ever after.

That is, unless Princess Ginevra of Norumbega had something to say about it.

Acknowledgments

Anyone who says that writing is a solitary occupation never had the pleasure of working with the team that created *Marabel*! This book feels like a real collaboration.

First, and always, my deepest gratitude to my agent, Lara Perkins, for her creativity, professional insight, and good cheer throughout the process.

Many thanks to the Alloy team: Annie Stone, Joelle Hobeika, Hayley Wagreich, Les Morgenstein, Josh Bank, and Sara Shandler. Every writer I know who has worked with Alloy told me that I'd have a great time with them and learn a lot—right on both counts! I'm also fortunate to have art director Mallory Griggs and managing editor Romy Golan steering the ship.

Many thanks are due to the Little, Brown team, especially Lisa Yoskowitz and her assistant, Hallie Tibbetts, and Allison Moore, who have fine-tuned the story and encouraged me to dig deeper. Thanks also to Marcie Lawrence, Sasha Illingworth, Emilie Polster, Jennifer McClelland-Smith, Kristina Pisciotta, Elisabeth Ferrari, Adrian Palacios, Victoria Stapleton, and Jenny Choy, and to Sara Gianassi for her wonderful illustrations.

Grateful thanks to the Society of Children's Book Writers and Illustrators for the education and support over the years.

A big thank-you to the members of my critique group (Shirley Amitrano, Mary Buckner, Candie Moonshower, Carol Stice, and Cheryl Zach), who listened to the entire first draft and then some, and who laughed in all the right places and have thoughtful and important feedback.

As always, thanks and love to Greg.